"It would take a whole lot more than treats to make your behavior fit my standards, Alex Norton."

But instead of being taken aback by her tongue-lashing, he stepped a little closer, eyes glittering. "What kind of more?"

Beth couldn't find her voice in her tight throat. He was here and close and she couldn't think straight. Her senses seemed on overdrive; there was a heady sensual scent in the air, her body aware of where he put those amazing hands now, wishing they were exploring her instead of shoved in his pockets.

She wanted him and she shouldn't. She'd immunized herself against him. She'd reeled from his words, nursed a broken heart. "A lot more than you've got."

"I can do more." He wanted to kiss her. She knew him too well to not misinterpret that misted look in his eyes. And hell, she wanted to kiss him, too. Just once. Just to feel his lips press on hers, just to taste him one more time. Then she'd turn and walk away from him. This time, she'd do the walking.

Dear Reader,

Many thanks for picking up *A Puppy and a Christmas Proposal*!

What in the world could be better than having custody of an adorable puppy at Christmastime? Unless, of course, you're forced to share the puppy with the man who broke your heart.

When Alex broke up with Beth eight years ago he thought he had perfectly valid reasons, and those reasons have been a closely guarded secret…until Beth breaks through his defenses and demands answers. Unfortunately for Alex, she is not happy with what he tells her! I'm sure they'd prefer keeping each other at arm's length, but sharing the care of a puppy gives them lots of opportunity to keep meeting up, until their mutual attraction reaches boiling point.

I loved revisiting Oakdale at Christmas! If this is your first visit to this fictional village nestled in the snow-capped hills of England's beautiful Lake District, then welcome! If you enjoy this story and want more Oakdale magic, then *A Nurse to Heal His Heart* is another of my books set there.

I love hearing from readers, so please get in touch via my website, louisageorge.com, or on Facebook: LouisaGeorgeBooks.

Happy reading!

Louisa x

A PUPPY AND A
CHRISTMAS PROPOSAL

LOUISA GEORGE

Recycling programs
for this product may
not exist in your area.

ISBN-13: 978-1-335-64198-4

A Puppy and a Christmas Proposal

First North American Publication 2019

Copyright © 2019 by Louisa George

Printed in U.S.A.

Books by Louisa George

Harlequin Medical Romance

SOS Docs
Saved by Their One-Night Baby

The Ultimate Christmas Gift
The Nurse's Special Delivery

The Hollywood Hills Clinic
Tempted by Hollywood's Top Doc

Midwives On-Call at Christmas
Her Doctor's Christmas Proposal

One Month to Become a Mom
The War Hero's Locked-Away Heart
The Last Doctor She Should Ever Date
How to Resist a Heartbreaker
200 Harley Street: The Shameless Maverick
A Baby on Her Christmas List
Tempted by Her Italian Surgeon
Reunited by Their Secret Son
A Nurse to Heal His Heart

Visit the Author Profile page
at Harlequin.com for more titles.

CHAPTER ONE

'DAMN SNOW. THE weather forecast said this Arctic vortex should have ended by today.'

Alex Norton locked Oakdale Medical Centre's front door and turned up his coat collar against the flurries that were now falling thick and fast, covering Oakdale village in a glistening white blanket. Winter had arrived with a vengeance with Christmas hot on its tail. And all he had to do was keep sane through the madness of the next month and then he'd be able to breathe properly again.

All? With the memories of Christmases past haunting him at every turn in this tiny claustrophobic village he'd be lucky if he stayed sane until the end of next week.

'Hasn't snowed this much in December for years.' His colleague and business partner Dr Joe Thompson grinned as he fell into step with him up the path towards the main street. 'Going to be a white Christmas, do you think?'

White? Blue? Yellow with orange spots? Alex didn't rightly care what colour Christmas was going to be, but he managed a half-decent, at least polite, reply. 'Who knows? It's three weeks away. This will all be murky slush before you can blink.'

Joe's eyes narrowed. 'I hope not. I promised to take Katy tobogganing tomorrow.'

Alex checked himself. Okay, so perhaps murky slush wasn't polite. Not everyone disliked Christmas, especially not the father of a pre-teen girl. Maybe Christmas might actually be fun with a kid around. *As if he'd ever know.* 'Oh, yes. First day of your holidays. Have fun. See you on the other side of New Year.'

'I'm grateful you've agreed to stay here to cover the clinic for us. Rose is looking forward to her first Oakdale Christmas and Katy's beside herself with excitement about the New Year's skiing holiday. For the first time in years I'm going to be able to get to all the school things they have at the end of term; the kids' disco, the Nativity… And she's going to love the pantomime in Lancaster next week.' Judging by the shine in Joe's eyes he was fairly keen about it all too. Which, as far as Alex was concerned, was a long time coming. Joe had been through a rough few years and it was good to see him smile. He figured Joe's new partner Rose had a lot to do with that too. 'It'll be good to be able to enjoy it all as a family without worrying about rushing back for work.'

'You deserve the time off. Happy to do it.' With a bit of luck he could bury himself in his job and forget it was the time of year that everyone seemed to go just a little bit crazy. Alex hated December. He hated Christmas. He hated the reminders of everything he'd lost, and at this time of year he was usually on holiday somewhere far away trying to drink away the memories.

But there would be no holiday this year; their other practice partner, Jenny, was off sick with a nasty leg fracture and their new partner wasn't starting until next week, and with Joe having pre-booked leave right through December there hadn't been anyone to step up but Alex.

Joe stopped as they reached the turn-off that led up the hill to his house. 'Coming to the carol concert later?'

'No. Not my idea of fun.'

'Good job you don't have kids, mate. You'd go mad this time of year with all the Rudolph the Red-Nosed Reindeers going on. Katy's been practising and let's just say that, although I love my daughter to pieces, even I have to admit she does not have the voice of an angel.' Joe laughed. 'Seriously, you should come.'

'With that recommendation?' Alex ignored the stab in his chest. It wasn't just a good job he didn't have kids; it was a physical impossibility. He dug his hands further into his coat pockets. 'No. I'm fine. A warm fire and a cold beer beckon.'

'The pub? Friday band night?'

'No. I'd like to keep my eardrums intact into old age. I'm just heading home. Just me, and not a red-nosed reindeer in sight.'

'Okay. So basically it's "Bah, humbug" and all that?'

'Yeah. Something like that.' Joe clearly wasn't getting the 'don't push it' vibe Alex was sending him. 'Enjoy the concert.'

'I'll try…' Joe grinned and waved his phone earbuds '…not to listen too hard.'

Then it was just Alex and the crunch of fresh snow as he stalked across the empty village square. Each footstep a beat…warm…fire… cold…beer… Warm…fire. Cold…beer. Nothing better after a busy work week.

Despite the streetlights it was dark and fresh and he wished he'd dressed more suitably for a blizzard. Every shopfront had some sort of festive display or Nativity scene and someone had strung bunting made out of silver stars zigzagging from the post office to the butcher's and over to the newsagent's. There was a small and slightly gravelly snowman outside the little supermarket, its carrot nose lying on the snow-covered ground. Alex picked it up, stuck it back onto the large white head and tightened the woolly scarf round the join between head and body. 'There you go, mate, whole again.'

He tried hard not to think how that might feel. But at least he'd fixed the snowman. See? What was that if it wasn't embracing the Christmas spirit? *Bah, humbug, indeed.*

He made his way down the icy path towards the opposite end of the village to where Joe was heading, to the house he'd grown up in, his thoughts tumbling between the usual tumult of GP life and that one Christmas eight years ago when his life had changed for ever.

He tried to push the memories away but there was something about those Nativity scenes that seemed to lock them in his head; the doctor's office decorated in tinsel for festive fun, diametrically opposed to the hot panic that had consumed him. The phone call. Tears. So many tears. And then navigating an entirely different landscape from the future he'd been planning.

From somewhere he heard a little whine, then an excited yelp tugged him back to today, the past receding a little. Behind him was a fluffy bundle of fur on four legs. Not a red-nosed reindeer but a dog…a puppy to be exact. It stopped

walking when he did. When he started again it
let out another yelp then bounded through the
drifts and caught him up, tangling between his
legs.

Huffing out a breath, Alex disentangled himself from the pup. Along with huge soppy eyes
it had a long snout, big paws completely out of
whack with its body and a tail that stood up like
a spike. Cute. If you were the dog-loving type.
Alex wasn't. Especially when they hindered your
journey home after a long day looking after particularly difficult patients. He stepped over the
mutt. 'Whoa, puppy. It's too slippery out here to
be doing that.'

It didn't move. 'Go.'

Nah. Nothing. He picked it up, turned it
around and plopped it back onto the snow, hoping it would return to wherever it had come from,
then he set off in the direction of home. *Warm
fire. Cold beer. Warm fire. Cold beer.*

Another yelp. A little bark. Did that one sound
like, *Hey, Mr Bah Humbug, I'm freezing*?

'Look, stop following me. Go home, boy…or
girl…' He couldn't tell from this distance. But
the puppy just tipped its head to one side and
looked at him. 'Go. Shoo.'

Pointy ears pricked. Well, one did; the right
ear had a floppy fold. One up, one bent.

Not cute at all. Really. Not cute.

And lost. He looked at the trail of puppy paw prints in the snow and sighed as he bent down. 'Okay, okay. Let's have a look at you.'

No collar. *Great.* A boy pup. And very happy to be given attention. 'Someone, somewhere is going to be missing you. How about you turn right around and go back where you came from?' But he couldn't help sinking his fingers in the fur at the back of the pup's neck and giving him a good scratch. The puppy nuzzled against his arm and something in Alex's chest squeezed.

No. 'I am not going to be bamboozled by big soppy brown eyes and cold paws.'

No. Nope. No way. *Niet.*

As soon as this silly season was over he was booking a holiday. A climbing holiday perhaps where he could put all his energy into something physical. A holiday fling maybe? That could be good respite too. A something with someone who didn't want for ever. He noticed his fingers were still fur-deep and his palm was wet with over-enthusiastic licks. It actually felt kind of nice. When was the last time he'd made a meaningful connection?

He didn't want to think about that, because making connections deeper than the ten-minute appointments with his patients was something he avoided at all costs. Dragging his hand away from the fur ball, he tried to sound authoritarian. 'Don't go getting attached to me. Off you go.'

He started to walk away. *Don't look back. Don't look back.* Words he'd repeated over and over to himself so many times in his life; in the darkest times, when he'd faced an uncertain future, he'd known that looking back at all those unfulfilled plans he'd made would have given him no solace at all.

But the puppy ran along next to him, sinking deep into the snow, then pushing with those huge paws and jumping out and into the next drift. 'A puppy with authority issues. I see. Just my luck, right? Look, mate, this isn't going to work. I'm just not that into you.'

The wind picked up as he reached his cottage, swirling snowflakes faster and thicker. He slid the key into the lock and pushed through into the cold and dark, pausing for a moment to stamp the snow from his boots. Wishing he'd left either a light or central heating on, he flicked on a switch, flooding the hallway in a soft cream glow, and caught a spiky tail disappearing into his kitchen. 'What? Hey! Houdini! You don't live here.'

The damned thing had snuck in with him and was now, he discovered as he rounded the corner into his large kitchen-dining room, lying on his grandparents' heirloom rug in front of the dining table, chewing on Alex's best, top-of-the-range and shipped-all-the-way-from-the-States climbing shoes.

'Hey! Hey! No! They cost a fortune! Let go.' A throaty, playful growl came from the dog as Alex took hold of his shoe and tried to tug it out of its mouth. 'I only just bought them. I've only worn them once.'

But the dog stuck his bottom in the air and laid his enormous paws out in front and kept on tugging back, that tail wagging back and forth like a metronome on heat.

'This is not a game.' Alex needed to distract it. 'Food? What could you have? Water? Yes. Water.'

He filled an old porcelain Willow Pattern bowl that had belonged to his grandmother and put it on the floor, then microwaved the sausages he'd planned to eat for dinner and chopped them up. 'Your last supper, matey. Then you're back out there.'

He looked out of the window at the whirls of snowflakes, heavier and thicker than he'd seen in a long time. Then he looked at the puppy, who was devouring the food as if it hadn't eaten in days. Maybe it hadn't. 'Who do you belong to?'

One tentative sniff of the sausages and Spike gobbled the lot—okay, so the name just came to him. It fitted the mutt perfectly, especially with

the tail that stuck straight up. And so much for
not getting involved. As a rural GP he'd been
around enough farmers to know you didn't name
things you didn't want to get attached to.

Then *Spike* bounded over to him, dragging the
now mauled and mangled shoe. Alex used his
best authoritative voice. 'Drop. Drop.'

But Spike went right on chewing at Alex's
feet. Whoever owned him scored very low in
the puppy-training ranks.

'You must belong to someone. Surely? How
would I find out? A dog like you shouldn't be
out there in the freezing night—oh? Ugh.' His
words stalled as a warm and wet sensation trick-
led down his ankle.

'Oh, great. Just great. A puppy with authority
issues and a weak bladder. Brilliant.' He looked
down and his eyes met those dark brown soulful
ones. He ignored the squeeze in his chest. 'Spike,
my man. Just what the hell am I supposed to do
with you?'

Sometimes folks loved their pets more than people, and Beth Masters understood that more than
most. Pets didn't break promises or let you down.
Pets never gave you the cold shoulder or silent
treatment. Except for the one she was examining
now; the poor farm dog was so ill, and exhausted
from being sick, she could barely move. 'How

long has she been like this?' Beth asked Meg's owner, local farmer Dennis Blakely.

The old man just shrugged as he stared down at his lovely old collie and stroked her muzzle. 'Help her, Beth.'

Beth recapped what he'd told her when he'd rushed through the door a few minutes before, frantic for help. 'So, we have a history of vomiting and shaking…like a seizure?'

'Yes. No. Well…she was shaking and coughing and then she was sick. It was dark-coloured.'

'Blood perhaps?' Beth did not like the sound of that. 'And now she's just completely exhausted. It could be a bug, or something she's eaten. Or any number of things.' Or, most likely some kind of tumour in a dog of such advanced age. But Beth knew better than to jump to conclusions and she couldn't feel any obvious mass.

Mr Blakely tore his eyes away from the dog and looked over at Beth. 'Something she's eaten? Do you think so? What kind of thing?'

Beth listened to the dog's heart. 'At this time of year it's usually chocolate. People leave it wrapped up underneath the Christmas tree and forget it's dangerous to dogs. Oh. Oh, dear, poor you.' She rubbed gently as the dog vomited onto the counter. This wasn't looking good. But she could see it wasn't chocolate that had made the poor pooch sick. Meg whined and laid her head onto her paws, her eyes looking deep into Beth's heart. Wait…there was a tinge of yellow in the dog's sclera. Liver problems maybe?

Her phone vibrated on the desk in the corner of the room. She ignored it. If it was urgent they'd call back.

They did. Her heart thumped as the vibrations made the phone dance across the wood. 'Excuse me, I need to get this.'

But it was just a text from her mother reminding her about the carol concert they'd planned to go to later. Well, that plan was about to go south; she couldn't leave poor Meg like this. 'Mr Blakely… Dennis… I'm so sorry that Meg is so sick. I'm going to run some tests and, in the meantime, keep her as comfortable as I can. It could take a while to get her stable…if I can even manage that.'

'Aye.' He nodded. His pale eyes filled. 'Do what you can, love. But save her, whatever it takes. She's all I've got now Nancy's gone. It doesn't matter how much it costs. Just save her.'

Beth's heart twisted. Poor guy. A widower of only two years and, judging by the scruffy whiskers and the unkempt hair and dirty clothes, he wasn't coping well. But caring for a very sick dog overnight would mean she'd have to miss the concert and she'd be letting her mum down. Again.

Because the progressive rheumatoid arthritis had eaten away at her mum's joints and rendered her unable to drive without a lot of pain she was relying on Beth to get her to and from the school hall. Beth felt torn; promises were something she always tried to keep, but she couldn't not treat a sick dog.

'Let's see how she goes, Dennis. She's very sick and you need to know…' Her throat was raw. God, she hated this part of her job. She put her hand on his arm. Despite the thick old coat that hung from his thinning frame his papery skin was cold to the touch. 'I can't promise she'll make it through the night.'

The man just nodded and looked as if his heart was breaking. She put a drip up through one of Meg's veins and bandaged her paw. The poor thing barely flinched. Then Beth popped her onto a blanket in one of the holding cages and made sure she was comfortable and safe while Beth ran the tests. 'That should start rehydrating her and hopefully she'll feel brighter. I've taken some blood and will do some X-rays and see if they come up with any clues.'

Someone banged on the surgery front door.

'We're closed!' she called out. 'Dennis, you go on home. Try to get some rest.'

'Hey!' The person outside rattled the letterbox. 'I can see you're in there.'

'Still closed!'

No rest for the wicked. She tried to remember when she'd done something wicked and came up blank. Sure, she'd wanted to be wicked…lots of times. But she was far too sensible to throw caution to the wind. As a child she'd always been a little devil-may-care but being her mum's carer and then having her heart stamped on had curbed that a little. And now she was a very responsible professional, who could hear canine yelping and human huffing.

She sighed, because sometimes she was her own worst enemy, but she couldn't let another animal suffer if she didn't have to. She just hoped it wasn't another serious emergency. 'Okay. Give me a minute.'

Focusing back on the situation in hand, she double-checked Meg was stable then walked Dennis to the door. 'I'll call you if things change.'

'Good lass. I just hope I got to her in time.'

'Fingers crossed.' But she had a sinking feeling that it was going to need a lot more than luck to get Meg well again. She unlocked the door and opened it to let Dennis out.

'Hey, Dennis. How are you?' A very familiar voice had her heart jumping. And not in a good way.

Alex Norton. *Great.* She breathed out slowly, trying not to let her body overreact, or her brain for that matter. She had more important things to concentrate on than Alex Norton.

Dennis sighed long and deep and shook his head. His movements were slow and infused with grief. 'Not good, Dr Alex. Not good at all.'

'Oh? Anything I can help you with?' Alex smiled. There he was with the smooth, kind and concerned doctor tone. *If only they knew.*

He was holding a puppy, which was licking his neck. And he was smiling.

Alex Norton and a puppy and a smile. How could the universe be so cruel?

'I doubt you can help this time, Doc. Not unless you know about four-legged patients.' There was a crack in the old man's voice. 'Meg's taken a turn. She's not doing well. But Beth here's a good 'un. If anyone can make her well again, she can.'

'Yes, I'm sure Beth will do her best. I'm hoping she can help me out too.'

No. Please, no. The last thing she needed right now was a conversation with the man who'd stomped on her heart all those years ago and—unfortunately, for Beth—the only man to date who could affect her with a simple look.

Not that she didn't want to see him per se; in fact, he was lovely to look at. From being a good-looking adolescent he'd grown into a damned fine-looking man in his expensive wool coat and jeans. His dark hair was shorter than he'd used to like it and the odd grey strand was creeping in. His blue eyes were darker than she remembered and had developed one or two lines around them. He was broader too, his shoulders more powerful-looking and he was, possibly, taller than back then. But with him being six feet two his mouth had always been a tiptoe to reach.

She was not going to think about his mouth. Or his kisses. Or him.

So, while she didn't mind looking at the gorgeousness that was Alex Norton she just didn't want to lay her eyes on him. Because whenever she did she was filled with such a heady mix of emotions she couldn't sort through them. Although she knew sadness and anger were definitely the dominant ones.

'Hey, Beth.' His smile was still there…and something else. He wanted something and, because she knew him so well, she knew that whatever he wanted was going to cost her.

'Alex.' She aimed for the same amount of ice that coated the path outside the vet surgery.

He didn't seem to notice. 'I wasn't expecting to see you here. I thought you might be going to the carol concert or Friday band night at The Queen's Arms.'

'Interesting. You thought I wouldn't be here? Or hoped?' He'd actually thought about where she might be? That was unusual; thinking of someone other than himself. Despite her better judgment she let him in but only because he was holding a pet, and pets were her business, not his.

But she didn't have the time to play nicey-nicey with him, even if just looking at him sent her heart into apoplexy. Stupid heart to keep hammering a tattoo for someone who dumped her and disappeared into the ether with not a single look back.

'I did wonder whether you might be here.' He lugged the puppy up under his arm. 'Or whether you'd even be open this late.'

'We are officially closed. And I did promise to take Mum to the concert, but I can't leave Meg now—she's really not well.' Beth hurried back through to the hospital area so she could keep an eye on the old dog. The poor thing lay with her head on her paws, breathing steady. No more vomiting, so that was something. But she didn't look right. 'I need to run some tests. Like…now.' She hoped he'd take the hint.

'Would you like me to arrange for someone to take your mum to the concert? Joe's going. I'm sure he'll be able to take her down.'

Not good at hint-taking, then. For a second she thought about saying no to him just because that was how she was feeling. But saying no to her mum having a nice night out when she rarely left the house was plain mean-spirited. So, it looked as if she was going to be beholden to Alex Norton tonight. *The first and last time*.

She managed a brief smile. 'Okay, yes, if you could give Joe a call that would be lovely.'

As he called his business partner she took the chance to check on Meg again. She was holding on, but very weak as Beth did her vital signs. She didn't move an inch when she was put in the X-ray sling. Didn't so much as whine as Beth drew more blood.

Alex came back as Beth was finishing up another round of observations. 'Okay, done. Joe will take her to the concert and drive her home afterwards. He was more than happy to do it. He said he'd make sure she got back into the house safely.'

'Thank you.' That was something to feel less guilty about, at least. One good thing about being in Oakdale was that everyone looked out for each other, even though it could feel claustrophobic at times. Like, when everyone knew when you'd been dumped at Christmas and you had to endure those pitiful stares and sad smiles and you couldn't wait to get the hell out and never come back. Except, of course, when your mum needed you. 'I'll give her a call and explain why I'm still here.'

'I'll wait. Er…*we'll* wait.' Alex cradled the

puppy against his chest and stroked its back until it fell asleep. Beth refused to let the sight of gorgeous man and dog do anything at all to her emotions.

When she'd finished calling her mum he asked, 'Was she okay about it?'

'Not really. We were both looking forward to going together like we used to do years ago, but she knows my work here is demanding and that I often have to stay late, or even overnight. She's used to me making promises I can't keep. But then...we all know how that goes, right?'

Ouch. That was probably unnecessarily harsh. But when you broke off a relationship—an *engagement*—by phone call with no explanation, you had to expect the odd barb, right?

Geez. Beth closed her eyes for a second as she found some calm. It had been eight years. Eight damned years. She needed to let it go. In fact, she'd thought she had, until she'd come back to Oakdale to help her mum and found herself bumping into Alex at every turn. Ironic really, given that eight years ago, when she'd so desperately wanted to talk to him, she hadn't been able to find him, and now she didn't want to see him he was front and centre of Oakdale life. The sooner she went back to Glasgow, the better.

When she was able to breathe slowly again

she turned to him. 'So, Alex, why are you here, exactly?'

His jaw clenched and she wasn't sure whether it was a reaction to her short manner or whether it was something else. 'I seem to have a new friend.'

And why do I care? Oh. Why *did* she care? Because she knew deep down she still did. Cared enough about him that he made her heart hurt. Just a few more weeks and then she'd be gone and Alex wouldn't be part of her life again.

Then she realised he meant the adorable puppy in his arms, who had woken up and was licking Alex's chin and making him squirm. She scrubbed the back of the dog's neck and it turned to look at her, large eyes brightening at her touch. 'He's gorgeous.'

'He? You can tell the gender without looking?' Alex's eyes grew bigger too. 'It took me a few minutes to figure that out.'

'I can tell the gender by the way you're holding him.' She tried not to laugh. 'But, if this is just a show and tell about your new pet then I haven't got the time.' Or the inclination.

She had to keep telling herself she didn't have any inclination towards Alex Norton. Except anger. Was that an inclination? There had been many times, particularly in the first few months after he'd dumped her by phone, that her inclination had been to force-feed him the engagement ring he'd so beautifully proposed to her with. That was, if she'd been able to find him.

Alex shook his head. 'He's not mine. He just followed me home, snuck into my house and ate my shoes.'

'All very lovely, I'm sure. And you want me to…?'

'Take him.' With the kind of smile that had once melted her heart, and now did absolutely nothing to her at all—*at all*—he handed the puppy out towards her. 'He doesn't belong to me.'

'Nor me.' Shrugging, she looked at the cute little dog who had a silky coat and bright eyes that were adoringly fixed on the man she'd once looked at like that. But he was distracting. They both were, and she had to deal with Meg. 'He looks perfectly fine. Healthy and alert.'

'He is.' Alex craned his neck away from the puppy's tongue and grimaced. 'Too alert.'

'Alert is a good thing, Alex.'

'I need to find his owner.'

'Of course you do, and I'm sure they'll be very grateful.'

'Has anyone reported a missing puppy to you or anyone here?'

She quickly flicked through the notices in the large clinic diary on the desk. 'No, not in the last few days. A white rabbit, rather unoriginally named Bugsy, is currently AWOL, as is a Siamese cat called Marg, but no dogs.'

She threw him what she hoped was an über-efficient and over-officious smile that she knew would definitely not reach her eyes or exude any warmth or encouragement for them to stay. Whimpering came from the treatment room. Meg.

Damn. 'Look, I have to go. Meg needs me and I need some answers.' And not just about what was ailing the dog. 'You know where the door is. Goodnight, Alex and friend.'

CHAPTER TWO

BUT HE DIDN'T LEAVE. He just stood there open-mouthed, shaking his head and cradling the dog to his chest as if protecting it from her. Great, and now she was Cruella de Vil.

'Beth? Really? You can't just send us out into the snow.'

'Yes, I can. That's exactly what I'm doing. You live a five-minute drive away, Alex. You are not going to die of cold just going back to your house in a fancy-pants Mazda cabriolet.' And, okay… yes, she was far too aware of Alex's life and his penchant for red cars that zoomed too quickly down the winding Lake District country roads.

'But…what about this little one?' He held the dog towards her and looked at her almost as dolefully as the dog did.

Steeling her heart against them both, she peered closer. Maybe she'd missed something. 'Is he sick?'

'No. He's a handful.'

It was just a ruse. He'd come here to dump the poor pooch on her, but she was in no position to take on a puppy. 'Do you have a fire or central heating at your house so the two of you can be warm until you find his owner?'

Alex's hopeful smile faded. 'Of course.'

'Right. And you're a grown man and a medical professional to boot. You'll manage.' She couldn't hold back the sigh. 'This is not an emergency, Alex. I am not needed here.'

'Yes, this is an emergency, Beth. I don't want a dog. I don't know how to look after them. I don't have the time. I need to give him back to his owner. Think of the poor little girl who is missing her puppy so close to Christmas.'

He was standing under a swathe of the cheap tinsel they'd strung across the clinic ceiling in an effort to be festive. His eyes locked onto hers and for a minute she was thrown back to a Christmas years ago when they'd come back from their separate universities for the holidays and they'd decorated his bedroom and made love for hours. Then he'd made her a crown out of gold tinsel, kissed her hard, told her she was the queen of his heart and asked her to marry him.

And she'd been the happiest woman on earth for a whole year, until he'd unceremoniously knocked her off that throne and broken her heart with a single phone call. Then had gone travelling…without her. In breaking up with her he'd not only cut her off from him, but from his parents and sister too…the extended family she'd always craved. Because, of course, when she'd come back home in the holidays and he wasn't around she'd questioned them about why he'd disappeared from contact. They'd rallied behind their beloved boy. With a gentle sadness in their eyes, admittedly, but they'd rallied.

We're so sorry, but it's what he wants. We're sorry, Beth.

For breaking her heart?

He could deal with the dog on his own. 'Feel free to find the owner and be the hero of the hour. Why do I need to be involved?'

He shrugged. 'Because I don't know what to do next.'

'Have you developed an allergy to phones or something?' She shook her head. 'Call the rescue centre.'

'I did. No one's reported a missing dog and they're full so they can't take this little one. No room at the inn, right?'

She rolled her eyes at the very bad Christmas pun. 'The animal pound in Kendal?'

'Same. Full, no missing reports filed.'

'The police? Here—' Raising her eyebrows,

she thrust the surgery's laminated card of emergency numbers towards him. 'Call the local station.'

He took the card but shook his head. 'You know, you're not being very helpful.'

Say what? He had a nerve. 'Alex, I am always helpful in times of need. This is not one of them. I'm in the middle of something very important. I have to go to Meg—'

'But you know about dogs.'

'I know about sick ones.' That was a little disingenuous. She knew a lot about animals in general, she just didn't feel a need to abandon her sick dog to help Alex.

He shrugged. 'I don't know anything at all. He's not mine and he needs to go to his rightful owners. He hasn't got a collar so it's not just a case of picking up a phone. Maybe he has a microchip? Or what if he hasn't? What if he hasn't got anyone?' He almost—*almost*—looked genuinely concerned. 'What do we do then?'

'*We?* Oh, no. That is not going to happen.' She was not going to get embroiled in this.

'Me,' he corrected. 'What do I do with a lost puppy? I'm working all weekend. I haven't got time for this. Oh.' Alex's mouth crumpled as a stream of liquid left the dog and hit the counter, splashing Alex's jeans en route. 'He keeps doing that.'

'At least we know his urinary system is in good nick.' It was getting late and she needed to check the blood results and generally tend to Meg but she also had a duty of care to the puppy too. Or, at the very least, she needed to make sure it was safe and cared for, and that the person responsible for it had an inkling of how to keep a dog alive. 'Look, if you can give me an hour or so to get Meg sorted then I'll be able to concentrate on this little one. Why don't you go home and bring him back later?'

'I'd prefer to stay here. You have all the equipment. I have nothing suitable for a pet at home. Plus, he doesn't like cars, he howls like I'm trying to kill him. I tried to soothe him with some classic tunes from the nineties but that didn't work, and neither did Rihanna, which I don't understand at all, because when Rihanna sings I'm all ears.'

'Okay, okay. That's enough.' She didn't want to know any more, she didn't want to hear his voice or see his face or be subjected to his bad puns, because those were things from her past and she was working forward now, not looking back. She dug out a bowl and filled it with water, and another one with puppy food. 'Give him something to eat and drink then go through to the staff room and make yourself a coffee.'

And she'd make sure she stayed safely at least two doors and a corridor away from him.

'Thank you.' He breathed out slowly, relief flickering across his eyes, and then he smiled.

God, that smile did her in every time. *No.* She stood tall. She was immune. She had to be.

'It's okay, I'll just add it all to your bill, which is growing by the minute.' She watched in amusement as Alex put the dog on the floor and then proceeded to follow it around, growling every time it started to get frisky or inquisitive. He clearly had no idea how to look after dogs.

She closed her eyes and counted backwards from ten, wishing that seeing Alex Norton in charge of a puppy—or, rather, completely out of control with a puppy—didn't make her knees weak and her ovaries prickle. 'Why do I get the feeling that I'm going to regret this?'

'How's she doing?' Alex lowered his voice to a whisper and crept into the treatment room, almost fearful of disturbing Beth as she was so completely focused on the collie. But he'd waited and waited and now he was worried the old dog had passed on and she was in here grieving and dealing with it all on her own. But no, both vet and patient were holding on. 'I've brought you a cup of tea, Beth. Thought you might need one.'

As always, the sight of her made his heart stutter. Her long honey-coloured hair had fallen over her face as she titrated the IV drip attached to Meg's paw, but he remembered every detail of her pretty features; the dark brown eyes that were warm to everyone, but him. With good cause, he knew. The perfect nose and mouth that had a generous smile…mostly. Not tonight, obviously.

Yes, this was difficult. He hadn't wanted to bring Spike here, but he'd run out of options. And he'd hoped Beth had had the day off. No such luck.

It had been hard enough for the few weeks she'd filled in as the general practice receptionist when their regular one had suddenly taken ill, but he'd always managed to skirt past her and had tried to avoid any lengthy conversations about anything other than work. He'd breathed a sigh of relief when she'd left to take up a vet position here because time and distance, it appeared, didn't make you forget. Strange, how the body instinctively remembered.

She looked tired, but as beautiful as ever. Capable and professional and forthright, and still angry with him. Beth had always worn her heart on her sleeve and he knew he'd stamped all over it, so had no claim on her time or generosity. But for the zillionth time in his life he wondered whether he'd actually done the right thing all those years ago.

Yes. He had. He'd had to set her free rather than lock her to him and an uncertain, potentially very dark and bleak future. And now? Even though things had gone a lot better than either he or the specialists had hoped, he still couldn't give her what she wanted or deserved. But it didn't hurt any less to have lost her. Never mind aching for the body he knew that fitted so well against his, the mouth that was made for his kisses. He fought against the rising regret. He'd done the right thing.

Forcing himself to not look at her, he focused on her patient. It was easier that way, because looking at Beth made his heart hurt. And sing. And beat hard and fast to her rhythm. Life had definitely been easier without her around, but he didn't want to think about not seeing her when she decided it was time to move on.

He didn't know anything about dog care but Meg's breathing seemed less laboured than before. She appeared calmer and less stressed. But that could have been his imagination.

Beth straightened and drew her gaze from the dog. Her eyes were soft and kind almost as if, for a moment, she'd forgotten to be angry with him. She took the cup he was holding out and had a sip. 'Lovely, thank you. I'm parched actually.'

'I wasn't sure if you still took it white, no sugar.'

'Yes. Oh.' Beth blinked and just like that she slipped back into the woman she'd grown into whenever she was around him: guarded, professional, distanced. She swallowed and put the cup down on the counter.

Damn. He shouldn't have alluded to the past. 'How's Meg?'

Beth breathed out and he could see she was shutting him out. The warmth in her eyes slowly seeped away, her back straightened and she turned away from him. 'She's holding her own. Just. She's had a hell of a ride. But I've run the tests: full blood count, biochemical analysis and urinalysis. Done an ultrasound of her abdomen and then an endoscopy and it looks as if she's got gastrointestinal bleeding and some liver damage.' Her voice was measured and professional, as if she were giving a report to someone she didn't know. 'She's been in a few times recently, with the odd cut or weird symptom that led to nothing, and has no other significant morbidity, so I'm thinking she's eaten something. I can't be sure, but with the damage to the gut it's classic signs of ibuprofen poisoning. And if that's the case we need to keep a very close eye on her over the next few days.'

'Poor Dennis. It would be terrible if he lost Meg so soon after Nancy.' As if the guy hadn't been through enough already, having nursed his wife through cancer. 'He's not really coping, is he?'

'No, he isn't and it's so sad.' Beth gave a sharp shake of her head. 'I know grief eats away at you and sometimes makes you distracted, so I need to have a chat with him about whether he may have left any tablets lying around that Meg could have got into. People don't realise how dangerous some medications humans take are for pets.'

'I'm his GP. From memory, he isn't on ibuprofen but I'll double-check at work tomorrow. It's easily bought from most shops, so he might have some regardless. I haven't seen much of him recently, but he's clearly lost a bit of weight and he looks a bit dishevelled compared to when Nancy was alive. He always made an effort for her.' He wondered how it was to have a love that lasted decades. Then stopped himself from going down that track because it wasn't going to happen to him. 'Maybe I could be there when you have that chat. Give him a bit of support, you know?'

Beth raised her eyes and looked at him. He could see she was thinking hard about this. Was that because she didn't want to spend any longer than necessary in his company? Were things so bad between them that they couldn't even do a joint professional consultation? But she eventually nodded. 'Okay. Yes. That's probably a good idea. You know him better than I do. It'll be good for him to have someone there that he's familiar with.'

'Good. Let me know when you're planning to chat to him. Now, it's getting late and I wondered if you've got time to just wave your magic wand over that little guy out there and see if he has a family who are missing him. And I don't want to leave him too long on his own.' At her wide eyes he reassured her, 'I popped him in one of the holding cages with some biscuits and a toy duck. Yeah, I know, just add it to the bill, right?'

She looked at her watch. 'Shoot. I've been in here over two hours? I'm sorry. Poor pup. But I needed to deal with Meg.'

'I know you did. But if there is a family out there, they're going to be frantic. I called the police and there are no missing-dog reports. I'm stumped. You're my last hope, Beth.' He tried the smile again, hoping she'd at least smile back. Or even laugh. Because if they had to spend time together then he'd prefer it without the daggers and sharp words.

'We won't be long, old girl. Hold on for me.' She gave Meg a quick stroke then whipped round to Alex. 'Come on, then, let's get this sorted.'

Wow. No smile. Definitely no laugh. She really hated him, and he didn't blame her one bit. He walked through to the place where they kept the large crates. The little pup jumped up as they entered the room, tail wagging, paws thumping, and yelping so enthusiastically it tugged at Alex's heart. 'What kind of dog is he?

Beth opened the cage and helped Spike jump free onto the ground. She bent down and ruffled the back of his neck. 'This beautiful boy is the best kind there is. A pure-bred mongrel.'

He was so out of his depth here. 'Is that a thing?'

'Alex, really? It means he's a cross. I think there might be some Labrador in there. He has huge paws so he's going to be big, but he hasn't got a lab tail. This is more beagle. He's got the tricolour patching, but…' She frowned and ran her hands over Spike's ears. 'The ears are wrong…'

'Wrong?' Alex felt strangely protective all of a sudden. 'There's nothing wrong with his ears.'

'I mean the ears are wrong for a beagle. Look, these are pricked. Beagle ears are pendant. Well, actually…' she smiled and held up one ear '…he has one of each. I guess we'll know more when he's older and grown into himself.'

'I don't really need to know as I'm not keeping him.' He absolutely could not have a pet. They were too tying. You couldn't take a puppy climbing up a mountain. Hiking, yes, but not rock climbing. And nothing was going to stop

Alex from doing the things that kept him sane. 'Does he have a microchip?'

She ran a scanner over Spike's neck. Finally. Then she frowned. Repeated the scan. 'No. Nothing.'

'So, he's a stray?'

'Well, I'd say he's at least three months old and the law now says a *keeper*—not an owner—has to microchip. If he hasn't got one then either the keeper hasn't got around to it yet or chances are he's a stray, or lost or…' she shrugged sadly '…dumped.'

'Dumped? What the hell?' He wasn't going to keep the dog but, hell, dumped? 'In winter? At Christmas? What happened to goodwill to all men and men's best friends?'

'It happens. Rather more than you'd think. Sometimes the dog is too fussy, or too difficult to train. Sometimes circumstances change and they have no room for a puppy any more. Sometimes they just fall out of love with the idea of having a pet.' She pushed the pup's mismatched ears back and rubbed his muzzle. 'You are so gorgeous.'

She was rewarded with a lick on her cheek and smiled. Finally. But it had taken a dog and not this human to crack that. It bothered him that even after all this time he still wanted to see the pretty smile that lit up her face and made her eyes dance brightly. He should have moved on. He had to move on, because he'd given up his chance with her and, besides, she wouldn't want him again once she knew the truth he'd been hiding from her. From pretty much everyone.

She stood and wiped her palms down her trousers. 'You're going to have to take him home, at least for tonight. Bring him back in the morning and we can see if anyone's reported him missing by then.'

'I can't take him back there. He's already weed on the carpet and nibbled a hole through my best climbing shoes.'

'Oh, no? The horror! Really? That's nothing compared to what I have to put up with in my job.' Her hands hit her hips and her head tilted a little as she stared at him. 'A nibbled shoe? Poor, poor Alex.'

'Say it like you mean it.'

'I mean every word.' She shot him a look of disdain, but it was laced with a faint tinge of humour that gave him a powerful thump to the chest. Because he wanted her to forgive him for hurting her. He wanted things to be okay between them instead of this difficult defensive manner she took whenever she was with him. A smile was a good first step.

But the smile quickly faded. 'You know, Alex, I really haven't got time for this. You tried the

pound in Kendal, right? I'll call the one in Ulverston. I know it's a long shot, being so far away,
but who knows?'

He watched as she made the call and was
thrown back eight years. How, when she was
on the phone checking in on her mum, he'd wrap
his arms round her waist and hold her close. How
he'd run his fingertips over her freckles and try
to count them, and she'd laugh and tell him that
infinity was the number of freckles on her body
and that he'd never, ever be able to count them
all. How he'd nuzzle his face into her hair and tell
her she was the most beautiful girl in the world.
And she still was, without a doubt. Not just in
the way she looked, but in her compassion and
good-heartedness…if not towards him.

He jumped when she said something and he
realised she'd ended the call and was now talking
to him. 'The Ulverston pound is full too. They
said they're often the first place people ring when
they're missing a pup, but they've had no one
call them over the last few days, and definitely
not for a puppy matching this one's description.
They suggest you take him home and we'll try
again in the morning.'

'We?' He couldn't suppress his grin.

Her eyes blazed irritation. 'You. I mean *you'll*
have to try in the morning. After you've taken
him home.'

'I've just told you, I won't have anything left if he spends the night at my house. Can't you have him? You have everything set up here for a puppy. Food, beds...you.' A night with Beth? One more night?

No.

'No.' Her lips pursed and he was glad that was something they both agreed on. 'I stopped doing you favours a long time ago, Alex Norton. I can't have a boisterous puppy in here stressing Meg out and distracting me from giving her all the love and attention she deserves. That's just not fair. She needs peace and quiet.' She gave him a look that seemed to say, *Like me. I need peace and quiet away from you.* 'Maybe it would be good for you to think about someone other than yourself for a change and take—'

'Hey, I'm a doctor. I think about other people all the time.'

But that was what she thought. She believed he was selfish and self-centred. And he was. He'd had to be just to get through the months of debilitating treatment and recovery. But letting her go had been the single selfless act in the whole damned episode. He couldn't have let her go through what he'd endured when his cousin had been sick; the long hours at the hospital desperately hoping for a miracle, the despair at Mikey's suffering, the prayers and then...the loss of hope.

He'd watched his family drowning in grief that had been raw and unending and all-consuming and had known the moment the specialists had sat him down and explained his prognosis that he wouldn't put Beth through that.

Clearly not wanting to hear any more, she went to the shop section and pulled supplies out for him. 'Here are some training sheets if you can't cope with a bit of wee. Put them on a floor where you don't have carpet. Your kitchen, perhaps? Here's a bed for him, a couple of toys. Some food. A soft cage you can put him in while you're not able to watch him. Don't worry if you don't have the cash, we take all major credit cards.' She scratched the back of the puppy's neck. 'There you go, Button. Do your worst at Alex's.'

'How about "be a good boy"? Or, "don't wee on the heirloom rug or eat Alex's favourite trainers"?'

She eyed him wryly. 'I thought you wanted me to say it like I mean it.'

'I've changed my mind. And Button? His name is Spike.'

'He is so far from a Spike it's a joke. Look at those eyes—they're like little dark buttons.'

He couldn't argue with that. 'But Button is a...a feminine name and he's not a girl. And that tail is all spiky.'

'No way. It's a sickle tail not a spike.' She drew

shapes in the air; one arcing and one pointing straight up. 'Sickle. Spike. See the difference?'

He ran his fingers up the fluffy tail. 'It spikes if I hold it up.'

'Whatever.' She rolled her eyes. 'We'll just have to agree to disagree. Okay. Time to go, Button.'

'Spike.'

'Button.' She held his gaze for longer than they'd managed to look at each other these last few weeks and his body prickled with heat at her fiery indignance. Yes, she still was the most beautiful woman he'd ever met. Why was his body reacting to her like this when he knew, rationally, that wanting her was the least best idea he'd had in a long time? Eventually, she drew her eyes away and sighed. 'I can hear Meg whimpering. I have to go.'

'And tomorrow morning?' He tried to think about Spike and not about the prospect of seeing Beth again as soon as possible. 'I've got a clinic booked from eight. My patients need peace and quiet, not a boisterous puppy distracting both me and them.'

The corner of her mouth twitched as she registered the same words she'd used against him earlier. 'You're not giving up, are you?'

'No. Beth, Spike needs you.'

Both man and dog stared at her and he saw the

softening in her eyes and the moment she finally relented. 'Okay. Okay. Drop him off here first thing, before your clinic. I'm hoping Dennis will be here too so we can have that chat.'

'Okay. Sure.' He whispered to Spike, 'See? She's nice really. I'm *persona non grata*, but you're not dog non grata.'

He got an ear lick for that. And an eye roll from Beth. 'And there'll be reinforcements to keep an eye on Button while I try to get a little bit of rest between clients. And hopefully we can reunite him with his owner.'

'Thank you.' Without thinking he pressed a kiss on her cheek and immediately regretted getting close enough to inhale the familiar fresh scent. 'I mean, Spike thanks you.' He held the dog up to her and was relieved when it gave her other cheek a lick that made her smile— a damned sight more than his kiss had done. 'You're a star.'

'No, I'm a sook with a soft heart for a lost puppy. It's just babysitting, that's all. I'm helping Button. Not you.' Pressing her palm to the spot where he'd kissed, she shook her head, and he could see the warring in her eyes. She hated him but there was something else there too. This was as hard for her as it was for him, but that didn't make him feel any better. 'That. Is. All.'

CHAPTER THREE

ONLY IT WASN'T ALL.

Being so close to Alex was a whole lot of everything. A whole lot more than Beth wanted. The temptation to rail at him about the way he'd so callously broken up with her was sky-high, but she wasn't in the right headspace to hear she'd been somehow disappointing as a girlfriend, or that he'd grown bored of her, or that he'd found someone better... There were hundreds of reasons why people broke up, she was just a statistic and she'd do better than to analyse something that had happened so long ago.

So she wasn't going to let him get to her and she certainly wasn't going to allow thinking about him to interfere with her caring for Meg. She would ask him when the time and place were right. Or maybe she wouldn't give him the satisfaction of letting him know how much she'd cared.

So she did what she'd done for the last few

years and shut down the part of her that still ached for him and didn't allow herself to think about the press of his mouth on her skin and how, despite her anger and confusion, he made her heart race and her body tingle, and she set about saving a life.

It was a long night. Too many times Meg's blood results had shown her to be the wrong side of critical, and Beth had fought hard to keep her patient from slipping away, but she'd held on. They both had and gradually, in the early hours, the dog's stats started to improve.

It was still dark outside when the front door bell jangled, alerting Beth to the new day and waking her from a light and very disturbed sleep that had been punctuated by regular alarms to check on her client. She tossed the blankets aside and sprang up from the recliner chair they kept in the hospital room, checking Meg for progress. She was stable. Which was more than could be said for Beth. A combination of sleep deprivation and an endless intake of coffee to keep her alert when needed made her jittery. Not to mention the Alex factor.

'I'll be out in a minute!' she called through to Reception, and quickly glanced in the mirror. 'Ugh. You've definitely looked better, girlfriend.'

Her hair was a halo of tangles, and sleep lines etched deep into her cheeks. Her eyes were bloodshot and her skin blotchy. Did it matter? What mattered was that Meg's owner was here for an update, having already called twice in the darkest hours to see how his beloved pet was.

She quickly brushed her teeth and patted water over her eyes then marched into Reception, gluing a smile to her face.

'Sorry to keep you!' But her already jumping heart skipped a couple of beats as she found, not Dennis, but Alex and Button waiting for her. 'Oh. Hello, you two.'

Alex's hair was rumpled, his eyes were as sleepy as hers and he looked even more gorgeous than yesterday, reminding her of those heady early mornings they'd shared after long, late, sexy nights when they'd visited each other at university. In one hand he held his work bag, in the other was Button. He smiled, although it was a little wary, and put the puppy onto the floor. 'Morning, Beth. You look terrible.'

She couldn't help laughing at his audacity. 'Gee, thanks. You don't look so good yourself.'

'I had a very interrupted night. You? How's Meg?'

'Touch and go. Poor girl had a hell of a ride. She hated the activated charcoal, but it was essential to stop her absorbing the drug and damaging her liver and kidneys further. She was quite anaemic from the gastric bleed, so I had to give her a transfusion too, which kept us both on edge for a while as she didn't react well to it.' She bent to the puppy and gave him a good old tummy rub. He really was the most beautiful, happy boy and it was affirming to see something with so much vibrant life instead of Meg, who was possibly reaching the end of hers. 'How did you two get on? Did he settle okay? Did he sleep at all? What did he eat? Look at me, I sound like a worried mother. God help my kids when I have them, I'll be your typical helicopter parent constantly fussing over them.'

'Right. Kids. Yes, I bet you will.' Alex swallowed and his smile faded.

Had she said something wrong? Maybe the dog hadn't settled or he'd had as restless a night as she'd had. It would serve him right for all the sleepless nights his abrupt break-up and subsequent silence had given her.

But then he shook his head and looked down at Button, who, despite having no lead, was sticking very close to Alex's ankles and looking up at him as if he were some sort of superhero. 'He chewed a hole in my favourite beanie, did his business on my work bag and wouldn't sleep unless lying here.' Alex pointed to his chest, and she wished he hadn't. His shoulders were definitely broader than years ago and, covered in that thick wool coat, looked just about the perfect fit for her sleepy head. She imagined how it would feel to snake her arms into that coat and slide them around his waist...

He harrumphed. 'The soft cage was a joke. I put him in it, but he just howled and howled until I picked him up. He won't take no for an answer and I'm pretty sure he's completely untrainable.'

'Going well, then.' She laughed, even though he didn't. 'You'll be glad to get him off your hands.'

'Er... Absolutely.'

'Indeed.' She wanted to repeat, *Say it like you mean it*, but didn't think that was fair. Anyone would fall in love with Button and she had a feeling—just by the way Alex looked at the puppy when he thought no one was watching—that he was a little way down that path. Although he'd never admit it. 'His owner will be worried sick by now.'

'I called everyone again this morning. The police, the pounds, the rescue centre. No one's reported anything overnight. I've made some posters.' He pulled out some coloured pictures of Button with the word 'FOUND' and Alex's mobile phone number on. 'I'm going to leave some here and get the shopkeepers to put them up in their shops between here and Bowness.'

'Excellent idea. And I'll put the word out to the other vets in the Lakes area. Oh, and Mum rang and said she really enjoyed the concert, so thank you for organising it.' Beth mentally kicked herself—she sounded too prim and too polite, as if she'd never known him or loved him. But she couldn't help it; keeping her distance from him emotionally as well as physically was pure self-preservation.

He shrugged. 'Don't thank me, thank Joe. He did the chauffeuring. I hope she wasn't too upset about you missing it.'

'She knows my work commitments sometimes mean I don't get to keep family commitments.'

'So, is this job here permanent?'

Weird question. Although, maybe he was just passing the time of day. She didn't want to spend any more time than necessary talking to Alex, and definitely not about her personal life, but one conversation with anyone in the village would give him answers, so she decided she might as well tell him. 'I'm helping Mum sell the house. She's moving into Bay View rest home in a couple of weeks. The whole process has taken longer than we initially thought and I had to extend my stay here, which is fine by me, but I have to keep paying my mortgage somehow.'

'You've bought a place? Here?' Was she mistaken or was that a flare of interest in his eyes?

And by way of a very misguided reaction her skin heated in response. *No.* She was angry with him. He'd already dumped her once. She wasn't going there again. Pets were definitely preferable to men who broke hearts, a zillion times over. 'Not in Oakdale, no. I have a house in Glasgow and I'm heading back there on Christmas Day after I've spent the morning with Mum. She should be well settled by then and I'm keen to restart my life. Besides, my old boss is heading off to Australia for a sabbatical and he needs me to take charge. I had to let my job there go when I came to look after Mum, so I'm thrilled I can go back.'

Alex nodded. 'So, you like Glasgow?'

'I love it. Give me a busy city over boring old hills and The Queen's Arms Friday band night any day.'

A little frown settled over his forehead. 'You used to love it here.'

'People change, right? Let's just say I've grown out of Oakdale.' She hoped that by saying these things out loud it would put a halt to any further feelings she might have for him or the place she grew up in. It would definitely give him the impression that she wasn't interested in staying. She needed to get away, from here and from him, as soon as she could. When the front door bell jingled relief skittered through her. 'Ah, here's Dennis. Let's have that joint chat. I'll pop Button in the little pen over there so he can't get

into any mischief. Molly's due in any second.
She can keep an eye on him while we take Dennis through to see Meg.'

Dennis looked as if he'd aged ten years overnight; he'd clearly had as little sleep as she and
Alex had had. 'How's my girl?'

'About the same as when we spoke earlier.
She's not out of the woods yet, not by a long way.
The poor love is old and tired and she needs all
her energy to fight.' Beth's heart squeezed at
the love Dennis had for his dog and she glanced
quickly over to Alex. She didn't know why she
did it, maybe she just wanted…what? Cama-
raderie, a sense of something shared. He held
her gaze for a little longer than she'd expected
and she saw something flit across his eyes. A
softening, for sure. Sadness perhaps? And she
knew—she just knew by the way he was looking
at her—it wasn't all because of Dennis.

But then what? So Alex had feelings? She'd
never doubted that. He'd just somehow cut them
off for her and given her no explanation what-
soever.

She opened the cage and watched as Meg lifted
her head slightly and sniffed Dennis's hand, then
she rested her muzzle in the old man's palm and
the two of them just looked at each other. There
was an understanding between them, man and
dog, that she'd witnessed often between pets and

their people. She believed that dogs sensed emotion and they were hard-wired to try to ease the burden, by their nestling, nuzzling, or just by sitting stoically at your side through whatever life threw at you.

Meg and Dennis definitely had that connection and it broke her heart to think it could end sooner than any of them had expected. Her throat seemed to close over but she managed to squeeze her words out. 'She missed you. Look how she's perked up now you're here.'

'Come on, old lass, get better quick. I need you home.' The old man's voice sounded as rough as Beth's. 'Did you get to the bottom of what's wrong with her?'

'I'm fairly sure she was poisoned.'

The old man stroked the dog's ears, but his shoulders tensed. He said nothing but gave the slightest nod.

Beth carried on explaining in case he was just waiting for more details. 'Ibuprofen. It's a painkiller. I can't be one hundred per cent sure, but I think she ingested ibuprofen somehow.'

Dennis went very still. Poor guy, it was a lot to take in.

'I-bu-pro-fen,' Alex repeated the name slowly as he spoke to Dennis's hunched back. 'It's a very common medication that humans take, but can be toxic, even fatal, to dogs.'

Dennis still didn't reply.

Beth tried. 'Do you know if you have any of it at home, Dennis? Anything that Meg could get hold of?'

He rubbed his palm across Meg's back and made little grunts to her. But then he replied gruffly, 'Don't know.'

Alex frowned. 'I checked the surgery records and Nancy had some prescribed for her when she was sick.'

Dennis shook his head again. 'I don't know.'

'I imagine you threw out all her old meds?' Beth tried, gently. 'Or did the community pharmacist collect them? Sometimes they do that.'

Dennis shrugged and kept his eyes on the dog. The poor man was grief-stricken.

She caught Alex's eye and shook her head, trying telepathically to tell him to leave it. They weren't achieving anything here. She tried to infuse her voice with positivity. 'It's a good job you brought her in when you did. Any longer and she might not have made it. I reckon your quick action gave her a good chance of recovery.'

'Did it?' For the first time since Dennis had rushed in with Meg his eyes brightened, but not before a tear ran down his ruddy cheek. 'Did I save her life?'

'Well, she's not out of the woods yet, but you certainly gave her the best chance.' She put a hand to his shoulder and gently coaxed him away from Meg. 'I think we need to let her rest now. I have to do some more checks on her, so why don't you go home? I know you were up in the night, so you're probably shattered.'

'I'd like to stay if I can.' He looked so stricken she almost relaxed the rules about visiting.

Almost. 'I have a few things I need to do for her and the clinic's about to start so we're going to get busy in here. How about you pop back at lunch time?'

'Aye, I suppose. A farm doesn't run without a farmer. Although sheep don't move so well without a sheepdog.' His gaze lingered over his old friend.

Beth sighed. Living miles away from her home town, she knew how hard it was to be on your own, but she did have a large circle of friends she knew she could call on, any time. 'You have no one to help you with the farm? Family?'

'No. No one.'

So, he had no one to share this worrying time with either. 'Very well. You do what you need to do and I'll call with an update in an hour or so.'

They watched him go and Beth closed her eyes. 'Sometimes this job is so damned hard.'

'He certainly loves that dog.' She was aware of a change in the air and then sensed Alex getting closer. In times gone by she would have

reached for him and had a hug but now she just
clenched her fists and tried to put that single tear
out of her head.

She opened her eyes and took a deep breath,
stepping away from Alex and his familiar scent
of sandalwood and fresh Oakdale air. 'Right. I'm
going to keep Meg alive if it means I get no sleep
at all for the next few days.'

But Alex shook his head. 'Something's not
quite right.'

'What?' She bristled at his assertion. 'It's text-
book poisoning and I'm implementing appropriate therapy. She's improving. Small amounts, I
know, but at least she's not getting worse.'

'Hey.' His voice was suddenly soft and concil-
iatory but his frown told her he was trying to put
his finger on something that didn't sit right. 'I
didn't mean your treatment, or even about Meg.
I'm sure you're doing everything right there. I
mean there's something not quite right about
Dennis.'

Oh. That would serve her right for jumping to
conclusions. 'I don't really know him. I mean,
he's been in Oakdale for as long as I can remember, but he's always just been the grumpy old
man up at Oaktree Farm.'

'He can be very direct and forthright, I admit.
But he's always had a sharp mind and he nursed
Nancy at home for the last six months of her life,

right up until the end, refusing to let her go into hospital or even respite care because she wanted to stay in the place she'd lived for the last forty years. And at the same time he was running a working sheep farm when many men his age have sold up and retired years ago. There are no children to support him, no relatives. He took sole responsibility for his sick wife and he did it very well with our support.'

'What are you saying?'

'If he was so involved in her care, he would know the names of her tablets, right?'

Beth wandered out into the reception area and waved to Molly, who was talking on the phone. 'He's probably forgotten or trying to put all that behind him. And the names are confusing, aren't they? They're never easy to remember especially when you're as stressed as he is.'

'You're probably right.' Alex shrugged and walked over to the pen where Button was gnawing on a puppy teething ring. He absent-mindedly stroked the mutt as he said, 'I was just thinking, maybe he did leave some medication out and he's too embarrassed to say, but worse… what if he's getting a little confused or forgetful? What if he just didn't realise he'd left it out? Forgot he'd even had the tablets?'

'Are you thinking general forgetfulness or something worse, like early signs of dementia?'

'I don't know and I'm certainly not going to jump to conclusions. He's not the kind of man who'd respond well to me asking him to make an appointment to come to the clinic, so I'll pop by the farm on the pretext of wanting to buy a fleece or something and try have a chat and see how things are going up there.'

Surprising. 'I didn't think Oakdale GPs did house calls unless it was a medical emergency. At least, that's what the rules were when I filled in as receptionist.'

'Normally we wouldn't. But sometimes rules are made for breaking, right?' Now he was scruffing Button's neck and playing with the mismatched ears with a lot more fondness than he'd ever admit to. 'Poor guy's been living it tough and he's never going to ask for help, so we have to make it easy for him to accept it if he needs it.'

'Alex Norton, what with this and looking after Button I'm starting to think you do have a heart after all.'

'What?' His gaze collided with hers and he looked shocked, embarrassed and uncharacteristically off balance. 'No. I don't. I'm just trying to save the practice a whole lot of work down the line by helping Dennis now before it's too late. You've got to be proactive, right?'

'Aha. And sleeping with Button on your chest? How's that fit into your heartless excuse?'

He let go of the pup and stood up. *Caught in the act of caring.* 'Actually, it was more a case of *not* sleeping with *Spike* on my chest. Haphazard dozing, propped up with pillows and at high risk of being licked to death.'

She imagined him on a pile of pillows snuggling with the dog and her heart kicked hard against her rib cage. She ignored it. Tried to. What she wanted to do was ask him what the hell he'd been thinking eight years ago. Why he'd disappeared and treated her so cruelly, and why he was showing her now that there were still remnants of the man she'd loved…why? *Why?*

But this was not the time or the place and, even though she wanted answers, she didn't want to hear that he'd simply fallen out of love with her, so instead she tugged her vet hat back on tightly. 'Don't tell me you let a puppy onto your bed? That is not a good idea for either you or him. You have to set boundaries.' As she was trying to.

But he smiled sheepishly. 'What choice did I have? It was either that or be kept awake by the howling downstairs.'

'So, you'll be glad if we find his owner today.'

'Absolutely.' He gave Button a quick pat and didn't look glad at all.

'And if we don't? You'll pick him up after your clinic.' It wasn't a question, just an affirmation.

But he stepped back. 'It's Saturday night. Me and the lads from the climbing club are going to go to the indoor climbing wall in Kendal.'

'Now you have commitments you're going to have to rethink that.' She noted he hadn't said he had a hot date with a woman and chose not to note the shiver of relief skittering through her. 'If I have him all day then you're going to have to take him tonight. That's only fair. I can't have him bothering Mum and her place is a mess of packing boxes that he'll get into. Our house just isn't set up for a puppy.'

'Can't I just have him tomorrow?'

'I thought you were working the whole weekend? Surely it's better if I have him during the day and you have him at night.' And sure, she was setting herself up for seeing him at each handover, but there was a puppy here who needed caring for.

A hopeful eyebrow rose. 'Tomorrow night, then?'

'*And* tonight.' Button had started to whine so she picked him up and held his front paw out to wave goodbye. 'Alex, this is a baby. You can't drop him just because you want to go out with your friends. Imagine if you do that when you have human babies of your own.'

His jaw set at that, his eyes darkened and he shook his head, and for a minute she thought he was going to growl at her. But he took a deep breath and ground out through a very tight mouth, 'That, Beth Masters, is a scenario that will never happen. I'll cancel my plans. Just try to find the owner in the meantime.'

Then he grabbed his bag and stalked out of the clinic, leaving her confused and stung by his tone. For a little while she'd been impressed by his generosity and compassion, but she was seeing the true side of Alex Norton now.

And for the first time in a few long years she was starting to think their break-up had been a very good thing indeed.

CHAPTER FOUR

KIDS. KIDS. KIDS.

Every time Beth mentioned them Alex's gut knotted. He'd reconciled that he wasn't going to be a father and he'd worked through all of that over the years. But now, whenever she mentioned them she had such a wonderstruck look in her eyes that it brought back all their plans and promises, and he found himself reeling back to before the diagnosis.

She'd wanted a football team because she'd been an only child and he'd agreed to it because he'd loved her so much he'd wanted to give her whatever she wanted. Even now she talked about children as if they were a definite, as if conceiving was going to be a walk in the park. She talked about them with a certainty. She was going to be a parent.

He wasn't.

He wasn't going to let her distract him any more, either. The morning clinic had dragged on

and on and all he'd been able to think about was
the way she'd looked when Dennis had cried, and
how much he'd wanted to comfort her.

'What a busy morning, Alex. I can't believe
the rush we've had on. All those winter colds
and flu. Looks like you're fully booked this afternoon too.' Out in Reception Maxine handed
him some papers to sign. It was good to have
her back, happy and well, following her heart
operation. Things at the practice were running
smoothly. Not that they hadn't when Beth had
helped out, but at least he could breathe for a
few hours every day now. 'You look exhausted
already. I hope you're not burning the candle
at both ends? I know what you young, free and
single men are like.'

He laughed. If only he had the chance to burn
the candle at one end, but work and Spike had
him otherwise occupied. 'Actually, I had a very
sleepless night trying to entertain a particularly
perky young thing.'

'Oh! No! I do not want to hear about your
escapades.' She put her fingers in her ears and
laughed too, because not a lot could shock their
seasoned receptionist.

But just in case… 'It was a puppy, Max. Don't
worry.'

'Oh? Taking on a puppy is a big commitment.
Does this mean you're settling down? About time

too.' Something glittered in her eyes, something that made Alex panic slightly.

'No. It's a temporary thing until we can find the puppy's rightful owner. Actually, talking of dogs and owners, have you seen much of Dennis Blakely recently?'

'I haven't, but then I was off work for a while so I could have missed him.' She tapped on the computer keyboard and read from the screen. 'Not since Nancy passed away, not really. He's picked up a repeat prescription for his blood pressure tablets a couple of times, he saw Joe a while back for a cut on his hand…'

'Yes, I saw all that. I don't suppose you know of any friends or people around here who'd be able to look in on him every now and then?'

She frowned. 'Why? Is he okay? Is something wrong?'

'I don't know. Just a hunch I have. Could be nothing.' But Beth had thought along the same lines too.

And there he was, thinking about her again.

Maxine tapped on the keyboard. 'I'll ask around. He's never been one for friends, to be honest. Nancy was the one who did the socialising. He's always been a bit of a loner. Sad, really—he doesn't look his best these days.'

In that case he'd definitely drive by and check

in on the old man. 'Okay, thanks, any information is good.'

Maxine smiled gently. 'Oh, and the new doctor called to say he'll be arriving in Oakdale next Saturday and will be ready to work sometime the week after. So, there'll be some relief for you.'

'Yes, once I've done the orientation, which is enough work on its own. Let's hope he's as good as Joe says he is.'

'I've heard he's wonderful. You all are. Mostly...' She grinned, because pulling people's legs was her speciality. 'And, last question—if we get a quiet moment can you give me a hand to get the Christmas decorations down from the top shelf in the staff room? It's about time we made it festive in here.'

He tried not to prickle at the thought. 'Sure.'

'And bring the tree in from the back door. Ralph dropped it off earlier but he had to make a few more deliveries so I told him to leave it there and we'd sort it out.'

'Sure. Decorations. Tree. Yes.' It wasn't as if he had an aversion to the actual tree or the tinsel per se, just the memories this time of year brought, bombarding him with emotions he preferred not to have.

But it wasn't until the very end of the clinic that they both had time to catch breath and fetch the tree and box of decorations. As Alex carefully lowered the fir into a prepared stand, Maxine stood back to make sure it was straight. 'Can you give me a hand to decorate it?'

He fought the rising memories of Beth and tinsel and her wonderful smile as he'd proposed, and wondered how he could extricate himself from this without offending his receptionist.

But before he could open his mouth the door swung open. Frank Entwhistle, one of their regulars who had the farm next to Dennis, shuffled in. 'Doc! Please… Can you help?'

Frank's colour wasn't good. He was pale and breathing too fast and too shallow. Alex ran over and helped him into a consultation room. The very last thing he wanted was to decorate a tree, but he didn't want Frank to have to be wounded just as an excuse.

And he'd driven down from the farm to the clinic in this state? Those farmers were so damned stoic. 'What's happened? Take your time. Take a deep breath.'

'I… I…was…rammed by a bloody ram.' The man held his arm tight across his chest and it quickly became clear taking a deep breath wasn't possible. 'Hurt.'

Alex gently prised the man's arm away and undid Frank's wool shirt. 'Let's take a look at you. You're saying you were attacked by a ram?'

'Aye.' He grimaced and rocked forward, biting his lip. 'Grandson...was teasing it...charged.'

Frank's chest and abdomen were covered in bruises showing extensive blunt force trauma. Alex sucked in a breath. Nasty. 'Made a pretty pattern.'

'Tupping season's over...aggressive.' The old man closed his eyes. 'I'll be okay. Give me a minute...' He slumped back against the pillow.

'Frank? Frank.' Alex tapped the man's hand and got barely a weak murmur as a reply. He checked his pulse. Thready. Blood pressure dipping too low. Time was running out. 'Frank. Frank.'

'Everything okay?' Maxine was at the door. 'I heard you shouting.'

No. Everything was not okay. 'Phone for an ambulance. Tell them we have high velocity blunt injury trauma. Probable internal bleeding. No, make that definite internal bleeding. I'll put in a line. Bring the resuscitation trolley and ECG. This would be a very good time to have an ultrasound scanner.' And another pair of hands that weren't Maxine with her recent heart stent operation and arthritic legs.

'Right you are.' She rubbed Frank's hand. But the man was still barely responsive. 'Hang in there, Frank.'

As he waited for the siren Alex slipped an oxygen mask over Frank's face, put up some normal saline and administered pain relief while monitoring his patient's labile blood pressure. Just when he thought he'd managed to get it stable with the added fluids, it started to drop again. Which told Alex his patient was bleeding somewhere that Alex couldn't see.

He was preparing to insert a chest drain when the paramedics rushed into the room. Relief rushed through Alex. Many hands helped in these circumstances and this was a basic rural GP clinic, not a hospital. He didn't have the right equipment or enough qualified staff here to deal with such severe internal injuries.

He described what had happened and his observations so far. 'He's had a serious chest and abdominal injury. He's hypotensive. In a lot of pain, although I've administered pain relief. He has ipsilateral decreased breath sounds so I suspect a tension pneumothorax. We need to do a needle decompression asap.'

'Got it. Righto. Let's do it.' Andrew, the lead paramedic, set up and between them they slid a large bore angiocatheter into the left midaxillary fifth intercostal space. Blood drained into the chest drain and Andrew grimaced. 'Let's get him to Lancaster double quick.'

Alex nodded. This was not looking good. 'I'll phone ahead.'

Within minutes they'd transferred their patient to a trolley and closed the ambulance doors and Alex finally managed to breathe properly himself. Even if Frank survived the journey to the hospital he had a fight on his hands. These Lakes farmers were hardy, but he certainly wouldn't be dealing with sheep for a while.

As he watched them head off Alex wondered how Dennis managed on his own up at the farm—especially if his mental clarity wasn't as acute as it once had been—and how Alex was going to deal with the sticky conversation that might eventuate. And then his thoughts drifted from Dennis and, somewhat inevitably, to Beth.

As he made his way back inside the clinic he allowed his mind to wander, in a moment of pure selfishness and respite from the intense hour with Frank, to the gentle ribbing she'd given him over letting Spike sleep on his bed. She'd smiled and laughed, and things had slipped a little way towards how they'd once been and, with it, so had his mood. Simply, she made him feel better. She made him feel a lot of things: happy, hot, calm and yet desperate. For her kisses. For her heat.

And he realised with a sharp pang of regret that he'd never got over her. And never would.

But he had to, otherwise he'd go mad being around her. He shuddered as Maxine closed the door on the cold air and said, 'Just when you thought it was safe to put the closed sign up we have an emergency. It's a good job you were here.'

Alex refocused. 'Did you manage to get hold of his wife?'

Maxine nodded. 'She's out of her mind with worry, but got her son to take her over to Lancaster General. Thank God for family.'

'Indeed.' Unless you were Dennis, and didn't have one. He made a mental note to suggest the old farmer came down to the pub more often, or joined in some of the community activities—at least that way there'd be more people looking out for him. Alex knew only too well what staring at the same four walls day in and day out could do to a man's brain.

'Hi there!' Beth called as she breezed through the front door, and Alex's heart rate trebled at her breathless smile. She looked even more exhausted than before and about three times more beautiful. 'We didn't arrange doggy handover, so I wasn't sure what time…is now okay? I've finished and am finally heading home.'

She let the puppy down on the floor. It careened over to Alex and barked and barked at his ankles and didn't stop until he bent down and gave him a big stroke and lots of fuss.

Maxine clapped her hands in delight. 'How

gorgeous. And Beth! Lovely to see you. How's your mum?'

As they chatted excitedly and petted the puppy Alex made plans for a quick getaway. 'Right, well, I'll be off now.'

But Maxine frowned. 'You were just about to help me dress the Christmas tree.'

Finally, he had the perfect excuse. 'Not with a puppy. Look at him—he's going to destroy every last bauble.'

Beth lifted the box onto the desk. 'Now he can't get at it. Look, I really need to go. Mum's waiting for me. And I can't wait to get out of these clothes. I've been wearing the same thing for two days. I need a long, hot bath.'

The thought of a naked Beth sinking slowly into a steam-filled bubble bath was not the kind of image Alex needed in his head right now. 'Can we do the tree tomorrow, Maxine? Seriously, I have to get this little fella home and sorted. He's had a long day and he needs his rest. Like me.'

Maxine grinned. 'There's a man with the right priorities. Of course, we can do it another time. Puppy comes first, right?'

'Say what? Priorities? You've changed your tune.' Wide-eyed, Beth stared at him before slipping her hand into a large brightly coloured crocheted bag she had slung over her shoulder. 'Okay, here's a lead. I thought it was time we taught Button to walk to heel. Or, at least vaguely in the same direction as you, with a reasonable amount of control so he doesn't venture into the road. Good luck.'

'Whoa. You want me to do this? A lead?' He tried to attach it to the smart black collar Beth had put on the mutt but Spike was having none of it and playfully turned in a circle, chasing his tail, every time Alex went near him. 'Hey! Come here, you rascal.'

Way to make me look totally incompetent, dude. Why couldn't you have been here when I did the chest drain? I'd have looked a damned sight hotter then.

'Why don't you show him, Beth? Alex has to walk past your mum's to get to his house—why don't you walk the dog on the lead together?' Maxine had a grin that told him she was enjoying watching the interaction. She must have known about their past history—everyone in the village had known. His parents had reported back to him that their break-up had been hot gossip for a while. And yet here she was, pushing them back together.

'Oh.' Beth bit her lip and looked from Maxine to Spike and then at Alex. She shrugged, looking as if a romantic snowy dog walk for two was the last thing she wanted to do. But her cheeks pinked under the gaze of himself and Maxine and a very happy puppy and she eventually nodded. 'Okay, walk me to my house and then you're on your own.'

They fell into step as they crossed the quiet village square. A very slow step, as coaxing Spike to walk with the lead instead of gnawing it was proving difficult. Plus, he needed to sniff every step, plant, electricity pole...

The snow crunched under their feet and Alex searched for something to say that would generate easy conversation. He finally plumped on, 'How's your mum doing?'

Another shrug. 'She's deteriorating. This recent flare-up hasn't abated and it's really taking its toll. It's so sad, it's like she's fading in front of me. It's not just the physical, but emotionally she's fragile too.'

He knew well enough how dependent Beth's mum had been from time to time and how much Beth had had to give up to care for her. She'd almost given up the idea of going to university, but the specialists had found a new drug that her mum had responded well to, which had meant Beth could at least have a life of her own.

But clearly that drug had only been effective for a while. The pain in her eyes speared his heart and he wished he could do something to help. 'And you? How are you doing?'

She sighed. 'I feel guilty about leaving her. I

feel guilty about living in Glasgow, but when I tried to come back after graduating she was adamant she didn't want me here. But physically she was so much better then, she'd even got a man friend who was helping her and they were coping really well.'

It was the first time in a long time that he'd felt Beth open up and he encouraged more. 'How did you feel about her not wanting you here? That must have been tough after everything you've done for her.'

'Honestly? I did feel a bit hurt not to be needed, but also relieved. It meant I had a chance to do some living.'

He thought about the kind of living he'd been doing: working, climbing, random sex with women who just wanted to hook up—and that suited him just fine. He grimaced at the thought of Beth having random sex with anyone other than him. 'I don't want to hear about that.'

'Alex, *you* broke it off.' She harrumphed. 'I'm not a nun.'

'I know.' He wanted to tell her he regretted it all. He wanted to tell her how much he still wanted her. But he couldn't take that step, not when they were just starting to communicate again. 'There's eight years to fill in.'

She took hold of the lead and miraculously Spike walked by her side as if compelled by some sort of weird magic. Then she sighed. 'It's a long time.'

'We could try to fill in the gaps.'

'Why?' Her eyes crinkled as she frowned. 'Why do you want to know what I've been doing?'

'It's called being civil. Polite. Plus, don't dogs pick up on hostility? Spike's only a baby—he needs a harmonious atmosphere.'

She almost smiled at that. 'I'm not being hostile. I'm just minding my own business.'

'Beth. Come on. I just want us to try to get along.' He knew he didn't deserve anything from her and he was touching a nerve here, but he couldn't bear being close and not being...close. 'Spike wants to know all about you. Don't you, boy?'

She looked from him to Spike and rolled her eyes. 'Okay. I don't know where to start. Oh, yes, I do.'

Her eyes met his and for a moment he thought she was going to ask him why. Why? Why had he broken something so good? Their conversation back then had been inadequate and brutal, but he'd been too shocked to be gentle, too scared to be anything other than quick. His heart banged hard as he hunted for the right words, but she asked, 'Why did your parents go to live in Spain?'

Unexpected. But they'd always got along with Beth and he'd felt terrible when he'd asked them to stick with his plan to protect her from his illness. They'd protested that it was unfair, but he'd pulled out the desperately sick son card and they'd eventually agreed to abide by his wishes.

'After Mikey died my aunt Carol and uncle Seb moved to Malaga.' He didn't need to remind Beth who Mikey was: she was Alex's girlfriend when his cousin had been diagnosed with testicular cancer; she went to the funeral; she saw the fallout of grief. 'They needed to escape the place that reminded them of their son and start somewhere afresh. Their marriage was rocky and Spain patched them up. Then two years ago my folks decided they liked it there and moved over too. I bought their house because it's been in the Norton family for four generations and I wanted it to be somewhere Melanie could bring the kids in the holidays.'

'Malaga's nice. I went there after uni. Funny, I might have bumped into them all.' Her eyebrows rose wryly. 'Wait. Your sister has kids? I somehow missed that. My mum's Oakdale gossip's not as reliable as it used to be.'

This was good. This was chatting on a level they hadn't reached for a long time. Although the light in her eyes when talking about his sister and her children gave him a little pause. 'Yes.

She's got a two-year-old boy and a six-month-old baby girl. She's doing great. Her husband, Jon, is something to do with media in Manchester.'

'No kids or anything for you?' Beth's eyes grew bigger. 'I guess I'd have seen them around.'

'Not on my radar.' Was putting it mildly. 'You ever get engaged again?'

'No. You?'

'Nowhere close.' He shook his head, shocked by the relief at her words and yet lost as to where to put that relief, because it wasn't as if he could offer her a future she'd want. 'What's been happening in your eight years?'

She shrugged. 'Vet school. A stint in America at an animal sanctuary. Back to Glasgow for post-graduate study. A job. A house. The usual things. Mum's relationship fizzled out. I came back to see her just for a weekend a few months ago, and I'm still here. She'd pretended things were okay for too long and got herself into a mess. A bad mess, Alex. It was terrible seeing her in such a state.' She stopped walking and looked up at him. 'I just wish people were honest. It would save a lot of heartache and hurt in the long run. Right?'

He knew she didn't mean just her mum. 'Beth—'

'Oh, here's me.' She turned away from him and pointed to the house he knew as well as his own. How many hours had he spent there after school? In the long summer holidays when her mum was still managing a part-time job they'd hang out together there all day. He knew that the wallpaper in the lounge had been ordered from Liberty in London. That the back garden was paved because it was easier to maintain.

That he'd pressed Beth against every wall and kissed her until he couldn't breathe for wanting her. That they'd made love in the kitchen, the lounge and the bathroom as well as Beth's pretty bedroom that had a clear view of the lake. Of course, she wasn't thinking any of this as she said, 'I'll see you tomorrow morning for handover. You want to drop him here? Or at the surgery?'

'Beth—' He wanted to say…what? That he was sorry. That he'd been an idiot and handled things badly, but if he were in the same circumstances again, looking down the barrel of that same gun, he'd do exactly what he'd done eight years ago. He would let her go. And wish for ever that things could have been different in every damned way.

She was looking at him expectantly, for an answer, but he couldn't remember the question. She huffed out a breath and handed him the lead. 'The vet clinic is easier for me. Bring him down for eight o'clock. Thanks.'

Then she turned to go and without thinking he put his hand on her shoulder. 'Beth. Stop.'

She wheeled round to him, the cold night turning her breath to smoke that dissipated into nothing. 'What, Alex?'

'I'm sorry I hurt you.'

She flinched away from his hand. 'It was a long time ago.'

'I wish…'

She lifted her chin. Daring, proud. Her eyes blazing. 'What exactly do you wish?'

So many wishes—most of them involved Beth. Some were attainable, many just weren't. 'That things were different.'

She pressed her lips together and raised her palm. 'Don't do this now. Please. I'm exhausted and I can't… I don't understand what you're saying.'

Neither did he. What the hell was he doing? The last thing either of them needed was this. He tugged gently on the lead and brought Spike close, then turned away from her haunting eyes and the mouth he ached to kiss. 'I'll see you tomorrow.'

CHAPTER FIVE

THE BATH WAS WONDERFUL. Beth's heart, not so much. Questions and emotions see-sawed through her. Why hadn't she just grabbed the chance to ask him what the hell had been going on all those years ago? Because she'd spent years building herself back up. She'd done well, too. Until she'd come back.

Never go back—that was a hard lesson learnt.

What had he meant by he wished things were different?

And why the big heartache now? Why did he have to say that when she was already emotionally vulnerable? What with wrapping up her family home, looking after her mother and holding down a job that involved beloved pets her life was wrought with too many emotions as it was, without adding Alex into the mix. But ever since she'd come back home she'd tumbled from delight at seeing him, to sadness at what they'd lost, then anger and a desperation to move forward.

She'd soaked for an hour just to get some personal space and to de-stress after the trauma of Meg and Dennis. And Alex. But eventually the water had turned cold and she shivered as she went downstairs, wrapping her dressing gown tightly round her. She hated being cold. That Christmas when he'd broken things off she'd felt as if she was cold for months. She hadn't been able to stop shivering and shaking, not for a long time.

Her mum was in the dining room surrounded by boxes.

'What about this lovely dinner service from Grandma Masters? I'm sure it's worth something…you could sell it if you don't want to take it with you.' Beth's mum tearfully nosed her wheelchair round the dining table, which was covered in the contents of the old pine dresser, while Beth fixed a smile on her face. Downsizing from a three-bedroomed eighteenth-century cottage to a one-bedroomed modern apartment in Bay View rest home was hard work.

Sure, it was a nice dinner service, but for twelve people? How was she ever going to fit twelve bodies round her tiny table in Scotland? The last time the service was used was when her father had been killed in a work accident when Beth was six, and ever since it had been taken out three times a year, cleaned and then put back in exactly the same place to collect dust.

All she remembered was sitting in this room after his funeral, not understanding why her daddy wasn't coming back and staring hard at the dainty pink and blue flowers willing herself not to cry. Every time she'd looked at it since she'd had a feeling that life was unreliable and that the rug could be well and truly ripped out from beneath you at any given time.

It was difficult enough sorting out the remnants of her childhood without going through every single item and reliving the memories. 'It's tempting to say yes to taking everything, but I'm not sure it will all fit into my two-bedroomed terrace in Glasgow.'

Her mum wiped her eyes on her cardigan sleeve. 'I've always loved my china collection. There's pieces from both sides of the family and mementoes that people brought me from all over the world. If I knew you had it then it would make me happy.'

But would it make me happy? Beth didn't want the oddly painted china doll from Russia and didn't have much need for the porcelain Picasso mugs from Malaga—from Alex's parents, maybe? But she didn't need her mother's heart to break along with her own either. 'I don't know. Let's put it in the not sure pile.'

'Beth, love, the only pile we've made so far is the not sure pile. I'm hoping for a keeper pile soon.'

She was right. Beth had hedged about taking any of it. 'Oh, Mum. I'm sorry. I'm tired. Maybe we should do this tomorrow after work, when I'm feeling brighter.'

Her mum covered Beth's hand with her own very misshapen one. 'It's not just tiredness, Beth. I can see that it's something else. Something's bothering you and I'm fairly sure it's not just sorting through a load of old stuff.'

Oh-oh. Beth wasn't in the mood for a heart-to-heart with her mum. When Alex had put his hand on her shoulder earlier and said he was sorry and wished things were different her chest had felt as if it were squeezing so tightly she was going to stop breathing.

Worse, part of her—a big part—had leaned in to him, melting at his words and the soft pain in his eyes. She'd genuinely thought he'd meant it. For one split second. Then she'd reminded herself what it had taken for her to recover from him last time. She wasn't going there again. She found her mum a smile. 'I'm fine.'

'I know packing your life up is hard. You should look at it as a chance to declutter. I've been watching a TV programme about it. You can't move forward until you let go of the past.'

How to tell her that just handing it all over to someone else to deal with wasn't exactly the solution? Beth laughed. 'Hmmm. The only thing stopping me from moving forward will be the hours I have to spend on eBay selling all this stuff.'

But her mum gave her an 'I know you better than that' kind of look. 'It's Alex, isn't it? That's what's upsetting you, not this.'

'No.'

'Love, I see the way your eyes light up when anyone mentions his name. I also know what the break-up did to you. That Christmas you came back and barely spoke, you barely ate, I was so worried about you. You just sat in your room and stared out of the window.'

Beth didn't want to be reminded. 'Now you're making me sound like a sad case. I was a lot younger and naive then and I got over him eventually.' And vowed never to let a man make her feel so empty again. 'I was over him a long time ago. I'm a different person now.'

It was just that seeing him all the time was frustrating in the extreme.

'I know you are,' her mum said gently. 'You're strong and brave, and how you hold yourself together when you're dealing with those sick animals is beyond me. But you've got a soft heart, and all I'm saying is that it must be hard being around him again. Sharing custody of that puppy means you're getting too close.'

'I'm working hard to find a home for him. The puppy, I mean, not Alex.' Although rehoming her ex to Outer Mongolia was a pretty good idea right now. 'I've put adverts on all the community social media pages and hopefully someone will come forward and claim him. Once he's settled things will get back to normal again.' Whatever that was. And there was the other thing—when she wasn't with Button she worried about him. It was getting harder to stay detached. From them both.

Her mum smiled. 'There are a few boxes in the attic with the things Alex gave you. What are you going to do with them?'

She couldn't even face looking at them. It was stuff she'd thrown up there in her anger, hoping it would never see the light of day again. Did she want his eighteenth birthday card? The teddy bear he'd bought her to sleep with when he wasn't around? That beautiful engagement ring? Up the ladder, out of sight but not always out of mind. 'I'm tempted to just throw them all away. Fresh start, right? Moving forward.'

'Really? Even that lovely ring?'

'Definitely the ring. Just throw it all away.' Beth swallowed, pushed his face away from her memory banks and picked up one of the six white porcelain jugs her mum owned. All very similar, all very pretty, slightly different sizes, but six? There'd only ever been a maximum of three people living here at any one time—why did they need six milk jugs?

She'd come here for one weekend visit and now her whole life was upside down. Beth put the white jug down on the piece of paper marked 'SELL' and took a deep breath. Result. Maybe her mum had a point: she felt better just decluttering one thing. 'Right, then, the only decision I need to make right now is whether to have a glass of Chardonnay or a bucket of Shiraz. Want to join me?'

'I shouldn't…not really…not with the tablets I'm on. But…' Her mum pressed a button on the chair and an electric hum took her towards the door. 'Okay, darling, Chardonnay it is. And shall we watch the tidying programme to get some tips?'

'Definitely. I think we're going to need them. Some of us more than others.' Beth grinned, grateful her mum hadn't pushed her more on the Alex issue.

If only you could declutter emotions too.

Oaktree Farm was four miles out of the village. Up into the low-hanging snow-filled cloud and beyond. As the car wove higher through the hills the snow got deeper and the air colder—even with the very efficient heater in his *fancy-pants* red Mazda.

Alex smiled at Beth's description of his car. There was something about a woman who had no problem speaking her mind that kept him interested. She was a challenge, but then she always had been. That was what had attracted him to her in the first place. He'd been waiting for her to ask him about that phone call and he wondered why she hadn't. Had she groomed her heart against him so completely?

For the last four days it had been going round in his head and he'd wanted to broach the subject again somehow, but puppy handovers had been swift and curt and she'd found an excuse to leave every time they'd met.

His full body smile quickly morphed into discomfort. He should have kept his guard up around her instead of muddying things further. He shouldn't have opened his mouth and said what he wished, but there was something about Beth being finally willing to have a conversation that had lulled him into giving her more than he'd planned. He should have—

Suddenly the world swerved. *No.* It wasn't the world. It was the rear of the car sliding out of control. Black ice. *Shoot.* Heart hammering against his rib cage, he took his foot off the accelerator and focused on the road ahead, steering the car into the slide. Trying to. *Trying...* He dragged road-safety messages from somewhere in a deep corner of his brain. *Focus on the road. On the road.*

He was travelling sideways towards an oak tree. The road was lined with the damned things.

Faster...sliding...was this the last thing he was going to see? Oak trees and ice? Not Beth's pretty face? Not the infinity number of freckles that kissed her skin?

Focus on the road.

A dip in the road, then a rise. The ice. The tree. The road. The road. And...he came to a sliding halt.

Alex sat for moment and breathed deeply. Holy hell, that was close. He should have been focusing on the damned road. But Beth, it seemed, was with him everywhere. All. The. Time.

And now it was getting dangerous. So, he needed to be honest with her once and for all—maybe then he'd be able to offload some of the guilt he'd been carrying around about the way he'd finished things between them. Maybe she'd forgive him. Maybe she wouldn't. Probably not.

But even so, he needed to address the huge elephant in the room whenever they were together. He needed to tell her the truth. Then maybe he'd get her the hell out of his head.

Glad when he safely reached Dennis's farm along ever narrowing and increasingly icy lanes Alex stepped out of his car and breathed in the rarefied air. There'd been no other footprints or vehicle tracks on the snow and he wondered how often anyone other than Dennis ever came here. The farmhouse was made of similar materials to most of the houses round Oakdale— walls made of whitewashed, locally quarried large stone boulders, and blue-green slate roofs. Although Dennis's roof had some slates missing and the whitewash was blackened in places by dirt and neglect.

Alex rang the doorbell and was greeted with a loud barking. So, Meg wasn't the only farm dog to keep Dennis company. That was something at least. Even though Alex sometimes hated living in the claustrophobic confines of a small village and he often craved the solitude of the hills, he couldn't imagine being permanently this removed from people. There was nothing and no one for miles around, just an endless undulating landscape of white. Of course, it would be a different view depending on the season, but right now he reckoned the starkness of it would be enough to drive him just a little bit crazy.

As he waited for Dennis to answer the door he glanced right, across the slate courtyard to a large barn. The doors were wide open, giving him a good view of the contents: two large green tractors, a farm quad and trailer and what Alex thought must be various shearing tools. He didn't know much about farming, but it was clear the machinery was old and well on the way to rust.

Over to the left there was a sheep-dipping pen that looked like some sort of weird maze with its own moat, and beyond, ewes wandered in a patchwork of paddocks that stretched down the hill towards Oakdale village. After Frank's accident Alex hoped the rams were all fenced off somewhere. *Baa, humbug.*

'June. Heel.' The gruff voice made Alex jump and whip round. The door had opened and a collie with a lot more energy than Meg ran around Alex's legs, sniffing and whining as Dennis appeared in the doorway. June was a dog?

'Hey, girl.' Alex patted the mutt's head. 'Hello, Dennis. Good to see you.'

'Aye.' Dennis gripped the door handle. Knuckles white. Face red. Chest heaving. A little breathless, unkempt, red cheeks, which could be a sign of rosacea or polycythaemia, or just not enough sunscreen. 'Is it bad news, Doc?'

'No. I was just passing and thought I'd pop in to see how you were.' Truth was, the chances of Alex just passing were very, very slim and they both knew it.

Dennis frowned. 'Meg?'

'As far as I know she's doing okay. Discharge tomorrow, I understand.' Alex looked hopefully beyond the front door. 'Can I come in?'

Dennis glanced behind him, then back at Alex, clearly uncomfortable at his question. 'Why?'

Alex stepped forward. 'No reason. I was just wondering how you're doing. I know you must be worrying about Meg. Thought you might need some company.'

'Not really.' The old man pulled the door closed behind him, and blocked Alex's path. Perhaps the place was a state. Perhaps Dennis was embarrassed. Perhaps he was just a man who protected his privacy from nosy GPs who turned up on spec.

Alex tried to deflect attention away from his client. 'To be honest, I'm parched. Any chance of a cuppa?'

'No. I'm on my way up the hill.' Dennis scuffed dirty hands down grubby, baggy trousers that looked as if they'd been around for fifty years.

'Did you hear about Frank Entwhistle?'

'Aye. Rum business. But he should have known not to mither a ram after tupping. Sheep Rearing for Beginners.' The old man's eyes narrowed. 'You're not here to talk about Frank.'

Okay. Alex took his chance. 'Just wondering about the ibuprofen.'

'What about it?'

'Did you find any?'

'Come on, June, heel.' Dennis clicked his fingers and the dog ran to his side.

What was this dog-control wizardry? And what was with the question-dodging? Was there or wasn't there any ibuprofen?

'It's okay, Dennis, you're not in trouble or anything. We just want to help.'

Dennis shook his head and waved his hand as if all this was just a waste of time. 'And I just want to get on.'

It looked as if Alex wasn't going to get his answers today. 'Okay. If you need to chat then you know where I am. Any time.'

'I don't need a doctor. I just need Meg back.' Dennis's chin rose a little and there was a glimmer of light in his eyes. 'I saved her life...'

'You did. If you hadn't acted so quickly, she definitely would have died.'

'Aye. Now she needs to come home.' He stalked towards the quad bike, climbed wearily onto it and then called to his dog. 'Come on, Juney.'

As if tugged by some imaginary force the dog did exactly as Dennis asked and Alex wanted to question him about his training skills, because so far his puppy had done pretty much the opposite to whatever Alex told him to do. But Dennis revved up and steered the quad out of the barn, took a sharp left turn and off up onto the hill.

Alex watched him disappear but not before Dennis turned back to look at him. Twice. Something wasn't right and he needed to talk his thoughts through with someone who knew him.

Luckily, he knew just the person.

CHAPTER SIX

BETH WAS PUTTING the 'Closed' sign on the door as Alex arrived at the clinic. Her stomach did the same kind of funny little flip it used to do whenever she saw his face—anticipating his kisses or just one of his warming hugs. She reminded herself it was just a Pavlovian reaction, that was all. It would wear off once she was out in the snow and with distance between them. Distance, she'd decided, was the best way to deal with Alex.

But there was no avoiding him, so she searched quickly for an excuse not to have a prolonged conversation as she stepped aside to let him in, taking extra care not to inhale his scent or stand too close. 'Hi there. I'll just get Button. He's having a nap in the staff room.'

'Really?' Alex laughed as he stepped into the clinic. He had a way with him that was almost lazily confident. He wasn't easily fazed; he was comfortable in most environments. He seemed comfortable around her most of the time. There was little of the trembling she had when he was close, none of the breathless dizziness. There was little to show he was affected by her at all. So why did he wish things were different? 'The staff room? Has Spike been promoted?'

One day they might even decide on a name they both agreed on. 'No, he's just spoilt rotten. Everyone who works here thinks of him as the "clinic puppy". He has more mummies and daddies than any animal should have.' She escaped as quickly as she could and called Button out of the room.

The pooch barked excitedly at the sight of Alex standing in the shop area of Reception, looking at the toy section. Man and dog greeted each other like long-lost relatives and she dreaded to think how all of them were going to be when this puppy-sitting jaunt finished. Or when she went back to her real life in Glasgow without them. Or, without Button at least.

Alex crouched and scratched behind Button's ears. 'How was he today? He seemed a bit off his food this morning. Did he eat anything?'

'Pretty much everything in sight.' She laughed, pretending her chest wasn't aching just by looking at them. Not just her chest either; watching his hands move across the dog's fur reminded her how assured he could be...which led onto other thoughts about those hands. The way he'd make her feel as he stroked her skin. The hours she'd spent just delighting in him and what they'd had together. The sex that had been so delicious, so damned good.

Stop it. There was no point thinking backwards; she had to keep going forward. She swallowed and found her words. 'Right, got to dash, I'm helping Mum again tonight.'

Alex stopped scratching. 'Still packing? It's taking for ever.'

'Tell me about it. It's a whole life to sort through—these things take time. Plus, she's pretty indecisive.' Beth handed him the lead and the poop bags. 'You probably won't need them as he's already performed today. Okay, got everything? Bye, then.'

She couldn't believe she was talking to Alex Norton about their shared puppy's bowel habits.

Their puppy? How had her life gone full circle so that she was back talking to her ex-fiancé about *our* and *we*? The sooner they found a home for Button, the better. And geez, could she be any more obvious about getting them out of the room? She headed towards the door.

But Alex didn't move. 'I went to see Dennis today.'

'Oh?' News on Meg's owner was important enough to stay a bit longer for. She tugged her handbag straps up her shoulder and waited.

Alex rocked back on his heels and stood up. 'He's got another dog up there. June. Collie. Younger than Meg, I think. Certainly more energetic.'

'That's hardly surprising after what Meg's been through. But, yes, I looked them up on the computer system here. She's Meg's daughter apparently, and she's been in a few times too with weird symptoms, nothing concrete. No diagnosis. Just random things.'

Alex shrugged. 'She seemed happy enough. But he was acting a bit strange.'

That wasn't surprising. Dennis Blakely had always been…different, but her mother had always said that it took all sorts to make up a world. 'Maybe because you turned up uninvited?'

'Okay, I realise not everyone is happy to have me around these days—' He raised his eyebrows at her and she knew her attempts at avoiding any further meaningful contact had hit home. It wasn't that she didn't want him around—hell, having him around did things to her that only Alex could do. It just hurt to be so close, to pretend this was fun and normal and that their past didn't rush up in her chest every time she saw him. The good bits as well as the bad.

She raised her hand. 'Guilty as charged.'

He smiled. 'I am so misunderstood.'

'Yeah. Really?' Now would have been a good

time to talk about that Christmas, but she needed to hear about Dennis and make sure Meg was going home tomorrow to a safe place. And she was looking forward, right?

'Seriously, I was trying to give the guy a chance to offload and to have a quiet look around to see if he was coping up there on his own. It's about ten degrees colder on that farm, I swear.' Alex tugged his coat collar up around his neck and she was overwhelmed with the same sudden urge she'd had the other day to wind her arms inside his coat and press her body against his.

This couldn't be happening. She couldn't think about sex every time she looked at him. She couldn't think about how good the sex had been. She couldn't keep doing this to herself. 'Did you find anything to sway you either way? Is he managing? Is he safe?'

'His house needs some TLC and his machinery is decrepit, but I can't say he's in danger. He whizzed off on his quad bike like a seasoned pro. I just think he's a bit gruff and very private. Not everyone wants to socialise—even though it's proven to be good for mental health and mental agility.' He smiled as Button nuzzled into his palm. 'One thing, though. Dennis might not be great with humans, but he has complete control over his dog. One click of the fingers and she's at his side.'

'What? Like this?' Beth could barely hide her smile as she showed Alex the new trick she'd been working on with Button. 'Boy! Boy, come here.'

Alex's mouth opened as the pooch padded straight over to her. 'Boy? Since when...?'

'I'm trying not to confuse him by using Button or Spike. When he goes to his for-ever home they'll still call him Boy somehow. Like we do. Hey, boy. Lovely boy...you know. I just thought it best to keep our chosen names out of the equation. Now, boy, sit!' *Please.* 'Sit.'

Alex's chin almost hit the ground as Button sat on his back legs. 'Magic. Witchcraft. Sorcery.'

Now she did smile. Getting one over on him had always been fun. 'Yes. Pretty much.'

'Where's the wand?' He looked behind her back, turned one hand over and then the other, standing so close she could feel the heat emanating from him. She clenched her muscles to try to stop the whisper of desire spiralling through her as his skin touched hers.

'Don't need one.' Turning her back to Alex, she covertly took a dog treat from her pocket and slipped it to Button, then gave him a fuss. She wasn't going to admit to spending every spare hour here teaching Button. She certainly wasn't going to admit to the clutch in her heart every time the clinic phone rang and she thought it might be someone claiming the pup she'd grown so fond of. 'Give it a go.'

One of Alex's shoulders rose and he patted his thighs. 'Okay. Boy, come here. Come.'

But Button just sniffed around Beth's shoes and paid him no attention.

Alex laughed. 'I think I need your invisible wand, Beth. He's certainly not bewitched by me.'

'Aww, one teeny, weeny hiccup and you're giving up?'

He took the bait, lowering his voice. 'Not a chance. He just needs a firm command. Right? Boy! Come here. Come.'

Button tilted his head to one side, one ear pricked, one floppy, and didn't move one inch. She could have kissed him. The dog. Not the man.

Okay, maybe the man.

Definitely the man.

'Boy!' She grabbed a handful of treats and closed her fist, called Button over and he came at her first command. Then she opened her fist and showed Alex. 'Not magic. Bribery.'

His smile grew. 'Cheating, more like.'

'Also known as training. This kind of thing takes time—you have to repeat and repeat and repeat until it's Pavlovian.' Like her tummy flip whenever he was close. Okay, so that had taken years to perfect…and she couldn't expect it to diminish just because her head told her body to stop. 'I bet Dennis has spent literally hours, days even, training his dogs. I bet it's not something you could do, you're too impatient. You always wanted everything *now*.'

'Beth Masters, I am not impatient.' He stroked Button's head then lifted the floppy ear and whispered, loud enough for Beth to hear, 'Don't listen to her. It's all lies. I am patience personified.'

She rolled her eyes and laughed. 'Really? I remember that spring bank holiday when you'd been given a surprise weekend off. Within minutes of leaving the ward you decided to visit me in Glasgow. You were supposed to be coming up the weekend after, but you just appeared on my doorstep saying you couldn't wait another week.'

'I needed to see you. Three-day weekends are the best.' He smiled some more…this time it was open and unguarded and sexy as hell. 'Best—'

'Spent in bed.' She finished the phrase for him and then wished she hadn't. Her chest felt as if it were cracking open as she remembered opening the door to him holding a bunch of drooping daffodils and a bottle of wine. Before she'd managed to say a word he'd pressed her against the front door and kissed her so hard she'd thought she was going to die of lust right there, in his arms. She'd never been so pleased to see anyone in her life, and she'd never been so turned on. Just the thought of it had desire prickling over her skin. She tried to swallow it away and rubbed her palms down her thighs to feel something other than a sensual ache. 'Anyway. That's how you train a puppy. Reward him for good behaviour.'

'Is that how you train humans too?'

'It would take a whole lot more than treats to make your behaviour fit my standards, Alex Norton.'

But instead of being taken aback by her tongue lashing he stepped a little closer, eyes glittering. 'What kind of more?'

She couldn't find her voice in her tight throat. He was here and close and she couldn't think straight. Her senses seemed on overdrive; there was a heady sensual scent in the air, her body sensitive to where he put those amazing hands now, wishing they were exploring her instead of shoved in his pockets.

She wanted him and she shouldn't. She'd immunised herself against him. She'd reeled from his words, nursed a broken heart. 'A lot more than you've got.'

'I can do more.' He wanted to kiss her. She knew him too well to not misinterpret that misted look in his eyes. It had been a long time but she hadn't forgotten. And hell, she wanted to kiss him too. Just once. Just to feel his lips press on hers, just to taste him one more time. Then she'd

turn and walk away from him. This time, she'd
do the walking.

His palm cupped her cheek and his mouth was
so close all she'd have to do was tiptoe up as she
used to.

It was easy. So easy it was as if her body had
learnt it by rote. She put her palm on his shoulder and raised her heels. Touched her head to his.
Heard the sharp inhale as he put his lips to her
forehead. Relished the tight rasp of his jaw on
her cheek. His scent was almost a taste in the air.

God, she wanted to taste him. Couldn't stop
now...the memories flooded her. His caress. His
mouth. Him. The core of her heart. The beat. The
rhythm of her life. Her everything. She brushed
her lips against his cheek then stopped a breath
away from his mouth. She raised her eyes to his,
so dark, dangerous and piercing. Urging her on.
Because after all that had happened they both
knew this had to be her move.

She wet her lips with her tongue, felt his shudder. Heard the groan. Then she closed her eyes
and brushed her mouth on his. Not a kiss. Not
quite.

Neither of them moved, but she felt the thud
of her heart mirror his. Could she do it? Could
she push harder, take more? Could she kiss him
the way she'd done back then? Could she let herself fall?

Then she heard her name in his throat, felt the way he offered it like a prayer against her lips, and she opened her mouth to him. He tasted the same and yet something new...of mountain ice and warm winter sun, of regret and hope that she felt settle into her skin and her belly and her heart. His scent, so familiar, enveloped and anchored her. It was like slipping softly into the past and stepping into a bold new future at the same time.

He put his other palm to her cheek and deepened the kiss, his tongue slick against hers, intense and intimate—only Alex had ever kissed her with such passion and it made her belly ache with need. She was kissing him again. As if the years in between hadn't happened. As if nothing mattered but this.

He slid his arms round her waist and pulled her to him. She wound her arms inside his coat and for the briefest moment she let herself fall into the feeling...muscled arms, broad chest, Alex Norton was more than before.

Before...before he snapped her heart in two and went loco.

He'd left her broken.

It was utter madness, going back there. Some sort of collision course of masochism. He'd already damaged her once. She was not going to let him do it again. She stepped back, struggling to catch her breath and pressing a shaking hand to her face, trying to take the heat out of her skin. 'Once upon a time I would have loved to kiss you a whole lot more, Alex Norton. But not now.'

He shook his head, running his fingers across his scalp. 'I know. I'm sorry. I shouldn't. We shouldn't—I just…'

Now. She needed answers now. Before she did something else stupid. She needed to hear he'd got over her and that this was just a little out-of-control lust that would fade the second she walked out.

She took another deep breath that eased a little of the shaking in her limbs. 'Okay. It's time… I've got to get a handle on what's going on here. You said the other day that you wish things were different. How? That you'd dumped me in a different way? That you'd been kinder? That you'd hung around long enough to explain a little more why the supposed love of your life wasn't for life, she wasn't even for damned Christmas? What?'

'Oh, Beth.' He held his palms up. 'You have every right to be angry with me.'

'Too right, mate.' The rage of old started to rise up in her chest, mingling with the rush of pure desire she'd had being wrapped in him. And now she was so conflicted. She wanted to kiss him, but she was, deep down, still angry with

'What?' That wasn't true. 'Please don't lie. Your mum said Thailand, I'm sure. Anyhow, you were travelling. You were taking a term off or something… It was so sudden and so unlike you that I thought you were having a breakdown or something. I thought it might have something to do with losing your cousin and you feeling guilty or depressed. But they were adamant you just wanted time out to travel.'

He breathed out heavily. 'Well, if you call being wheeled from the ward to Theatre and back again, then to Oncology, then to chemotherapy ad infinitum *travelling*, then I guess you could say I was fully immersed in the experience.'

What the hell? He'd been sick? Her heart contracted. 'Oncology? Chemo? What are you talking about? Your parents told me—'

He pulled out a chair from behind the desk and slumped down on it. 'I know what they said, Beth, because I told them to say that. I didn't want you to know the truth.'

'But…' She didn't even want to say the word, never mind think through the implications. 'Oncology?'

'Testicular cancer.'

'Oh, my God.' Her heart collapsed in on itself and she went to put her arms around him. But stopped, because she didn't know whether hold-

him. How could you want to kiss someone w
made you feel all mixed-up inside?

She fought it, because she didn't want him t
see what he'd done to her and she wasn't sure sh
wanted to hear what he had to say. Closure was
one thing, but actively putting yourself in the
line of fire was something else altogether. But
she needed to draw a line under the past so she
took a moment to control herself then said, as
calmly as she could, 'You dumped me just before
Christmas and then went travelling. You broke
promises and I'm still not sure exactly what I'd
done wrong. Basically, you broke my heart, Alex.
Why wouldn't I be angry about that?'

His eyes flickered closed. When they opened
again they were haunted and dark. 'I didn't go
travelling, Beth.'

'Yes, you did. Your parents told me. Thailand or something. I can't remember the details.
Hard to listen when your heart is breaking.' She'd
briefly seen them when she'd come back from
university for the Christmas holidays. They were
heading off now, they'd said as they'd bundled
suitcases into their car. *We're so sorry, it's what
he wants.* And she'd been left with a zillion unan-
swered questions and had gone back to university
none the wiser, and growing angrier by the day.

'I didn't go travelling. I was in England. London, actually.'

ing him now was a good thing or not or where it might lead or what to do generally. While her mind reached out for explanations and reasoning her body ached for him. She didn't know how to act, but she sure as hell knew how to feel. Right now, she was a mix of so many emotions she lost count. 'Alex, I'm so sorry. It must have been so frightening—and now? Are you okay?'

He nodded and there was a dim light in his eyes that told her he'd been through too much and he was welcoming the relief to be able to say, 'All clear.'

'Thank God.' She breathed out, not even re-alising her breath had stalled in her throat. He was okay. He was okay. So many questions bubbled around her head and it felt as if there were a heavy weight on her chest. 'But…like Mikey? You had the same thing as your cousin?'

She'd been there through Mikey's treatment, watched a vibrant young man who loved playing football and basketball, who loved music and hanging out, who had been just a regular teenager, be ravaged by the disease. She'd watched the family implode in grief. She'd stood by Alex's side through it all. It had brought them closer, that was what he'd said, and that she'd been his guiding light in the dark.

Then, when he'd needed her he'd snuffed the light out and lied?

He put his hands to his head. 'Sucks, right? Who would have thought that kind of lightning could strike twice in the same family? But, apparently, with some types of cancer there is a familial link. Only, I survived and he didn't.'

Certainly not for the lack of wanting, hoping, bargaining with whatever higher force might listen. Alex had been glued to his older cousin's bedside, had all but moved into the hospital to help him. He'd attended every appointment with him, asked all the difficult questions and had been there when Mikey had railed at the unjustness of it all. He'd sat up with him for endless nights, distracted him with computer games and talk of the future. But in the end, nothing had helped. Mikey had been diagnosed too late and not even his cousin's strength and hope could save him.

And Alex had been through that and told his parents to lie to her? She couldn't stop her hands from shaking. She suddenly felt sick. He'd been ill, so very ill and he hadn't wanted her to know? 'You had cancer and you didn't tell me? Your girlfriend? Your fiancée? The woman you declared to be the love of your life? You kept that from me? Who even does that?'

His features flattened. 'I did.'

'It doesn't make any sense. Why? Why didn't you say anything?'

He reached out and touched her arm. 'I had my reasons. I was trying to protect you.'

She shrugged away from him. 'That really is not how it works. That is not how love works, Alex. Not at all. You stick with them, you trust them to look after you, you let them love you. You don't lie and get your parents to lie.'

'I was in a panic. It was a shock and I didn't know what to do.'

'So you pretended you were going on holiday instead of telling me you were in hospital? Wow.' She needed to breathe fresh air. She needed to get the hell away and work out what this all meant. 'You broke me. I thought you'd found someone else. I thought you'd got bored. I thought I wasn't enough.'

'You were enough, Beth. You were everything.' He shook his head. 'I'm sorry.'

'That's really not going to cut it.'

How could she have been enough if he hadn't been able to tell her the most intimate thing he was facing?

Biting back the sting of tears, she stumbled towards the door, almost tripping over Button. And whatever else Alex might have said, she didn't know. She didn't want to hear. She slammed the door behind her and crunched across fresh snow, trying to breathe, trying to understand how anyone could do such a thing.

He'd been having chemotherapy. He'd been in hospital and she hadn't known. She'd imagined him on a beach with another woman, having lazy sex under a hot sun. Laughing, kissing, stroking. Loving. Only not with her. But the hard reality had been that he'd faced something utterly frightening and he hadn't looked to her for support.

He'd lied to her. He'd not let her in at the most difficult time of his life. It was cruel. Just cruel. He hadn't given her the chance to care.

That was all she needed to know.

CHAPTER SEVEN

SHE HADN'T LET him explain.

He tried. He chased after her, but she refused to speak or listen or stop. Since then, at every doggy handover she'd turned down any chance at communication and only gave him reluctant eye contact. He could see that even this morning, days later, she was still seething. She had good reason, but he didn't want it to go on any more without making her listen; he just had to work out how.

Which was impossible when he was currently the only glue holding his GP practice together and he had to focus here and not on her and his past. But his head kept on going there. Too much and too often. The kiss still lingered on his lips; he could still remember the taste of her, the way she'd fitted back into his arms as perfectly as before.

Kissing her had been stupid because it had woken something up inside him. Something that could never be a reality so he'd be better leaving her to stew and to let her hate him. But even if he couldn't offer her anything before she went back to Glasgow, he wanted to be honest and truthful and open.

'This is Dr Fraser Moore and his daughter, Lily. The cavalry in our hours of need,' Maxine joked as she introduced Alex to them in the clinic reception area during his Monday lunch break, such as it was—if he was lucky, he'd get five minutes before the next patient strolled in. He noted the clinic was now bedecked in Christmas glitter and tinsel and that the Christmas tree had been decorated. Thankfully, Maxine had steered away from asking him to help a second time. But just the sight of the tinsel had him thinking of Beth all over again. Maxine glared at him and gave him a 'go on, smile' kind of look. 'This is Alex Norton. He'll show you both round the practice.'

'Good to meet you, Alex. Not sure I'm cavalry material but I'll do my best at patching up the injured.' Fraser smiled and shook Alex's hand. He seemed okay. About the same age as himself... maybe a bit older if he had a teenage daughter. 'We're keen to get stuck in and get to know the community here, aren't we, Lily?'

The girl slouched forward and nodded. She

was like a Fraser female mini-me although where her father had short dark hair, hers was long and pulled into a scruffy ponytail. She had large dark eyes that, also in contrast to her father's, were not at all amused or brimming with enthusiasm. She wore a thick woollen jumper that was so big on her it looked as if it belonged to her dad and skintight jeans and trainers. The typical uniform of all the teenagers round Oakdale. As was the grouchy look on her face. No smile. No hand-shake. She just rolled her eyes and managed, 'Er...yeah. Hi.'

He wondered if there was a mum around, but it didn't feel appropriate to ask so Alex just walked them through the clinic, showing Fraser his con-sulting room, the treatment spaces and nurses' rooms. 'It's your average rural GP clinic, but things are getting a bit hectic with the usual win-ter colds and flu. There's only me at the moment, so I'm very glad to have you here.'

'Is tomorrow good for me to start?' Fraser looked keen. A good thing indeed.

'Tomorrow is great. We'll arrange a cut-down clinic after a morning orientation. Maxine will run through the software with you, although I think I read you used the same one in your GP practice in London?'

'Sure did. I've also done a fair bit of locum

work over the years, so I'm used to fitting in and working things out on my own.'

'Have a cuppa before you head out into that cold.' Maxine brought a tray with tea and biscuits into the staff room and Alex shoved back a groan. He needed to get back to work, but he also needed to be polite.

It was both a blessing and a curse to be so busy that he could barely breathe, let alone think. The weekend had been a washout, both weather and mood wise. Dark heavy clouds had emptied more snow over the roads and mountains, which had meant his usual weekend activities of hiking and climbing had been cancelled. Normally he used the discipline and concentration of climbing as a form of meditation to clear his head so, being stuck inside with a frisky puppy that seemed to have as much tense energy as Alex did had almost driven him crazy.

The only outside time he'd managed had been to take Spike out for short walks, between snow falls, around the low-lying hills. But, maybe sensing Alex's mood or the impasse between him and Beth, their dog had been particularly disobedient, except at their handovers where he'd been exemplary in front of Beth.

Which had made everything worse.

Not that much could be worse. He didn't know

how to make it right apart from more talking and she wasn't having any of that.

He turned to Lily, who was squirrelling away the custard creams. 'Will you be going to Bowness High School?'

The girl shrugged. 'The same place my dad's going to run the evening outreach clinics? Great. Can. Not. Wait.' Her accent was southern, London maybe, longer-stretched-out vowels, no northern bluntness. Except for in her tone. She did not want to be in Oakdale.

It was Fraser's turn to grimace. 'Sorry, yes, she will, after the holidays, no point in her starting just as they're about to break up for Christmas. She's going to be helping me out with sorting our things in the cottage.'

'You've bought? Renting?'

'Bought,' Fraser explained. 'Thought it might make us feel more settled.'

'As if.' Lily sighed and rolled her eyes. 'What's the Wi-Fi like around here? It's been rubbish all weekend. In Clapham it was brilliant.'

'Sporadic at best.' Alex caught the new GP's eye as he winced.

'But you won't be needing it as much, I'm sure, Lily. There's lots to do here.' Fraser sounded hopeful and Alex smiled to himself. If you liked the outdoors the Lake District was brilliant, but if you were forced to move here from a busy city—and he wondered if that was why Lily was so grumpy—and you didn't much like hills and countryside, then it was going to be a bit of a struggle.

Alex tried to help. 'There's a great climbing wall in Kendal if you like that kind of thing. And there's some very cool cinemas in Ambleside. Pop into the tourist information centre at Bowness—they have lots of ideas of things to do and they might know of some school-holiday activities going on.'

Lily sighed again and shook her head and Alex felt for both father and daughter. He didn't know their story, but there clearly was one.

Fraser put down his cup. 'Right, we're heading off to the school to sign Lily up then we've a few more things I need to tick off the list. Registering at the doctors' is easy, clearly. We need to take Jasper to the vets…do you know any good ones round here you could recommend?'

Did he? The best. He couldn't forget the image of her haunted face as he'd told her the truth. The hurt he'd caused then and now that was etched in her features. The swirl of tears that she'd steadfastly blocked away. And the pain under his rib cage that never seemed to abate. He'd do anything to take all that back, but she wasn't giving him the chance. He looked at Lily, who was staring at him as if he were crazy. 'Oh. Jasper?

'A dog?' she said, making it sound more like *duh*?

'Is he sick?'

'No.' More *duh*. 'He needs a haircut.'

And for the first time ever Alex was a little relieved that kids weren't going to happen to him.

Beth didn't want to talk to Alex because she was finding it damned hard to forgive him—or to even understand what the hell he'd been trying to achieve by lying to her—but here he was strolling into the clinic as if he owned the place and she had nowhere to hide.

Angus was holding the door open and chatting to him and she wanted to shout out to her boss not to leave her here with Alex because she wasn't sure what she was going to do with all the bottled-up anger, but she also didn't want to sound like a crazy woman.

She casually waved as Angus left and then pretended she was busy on the clinic computer, simultaneously trying to stop her hands from shaking and giving her away. She'd wanted to kiss him one last time and walk away unscathed, but instead she felt as if she'd been hit by a two-ton farming truck. And yet there were parts of her that still ached for his touch. Go figure. Maybe she was a crazy woman.

He came and stood on the opposite side of the reception desk, a face of smiles and sorry and all kinds of sexy. The kiss they'd shared, right here, was a spectre looming between them. 'Hi, Beth.'

'Button's in the soft cage in the treatment room.'

'Oh? Not the staff room today? He's been demoted?'

'Turns out he's a bit more stubborn than I originally thought.' Or maybe she'd been a little stretched and short-tempered today. The last few days, if she was honest—even her mum had commented on her bad mood. 'He kept trying to pull the food bags off the shelves and even got into one of them, so I had to put him somewhere safe while I worked. Anyway, you can go through and get him. I've got notes to write up.'

'Beth, we need to—'

'No.' She cut him off without giving him the pleasure or advantage of being in control of any of this.

She watched him disappear into the treatment room and put her head in her hands. This was too hard. Made harder because she wasn't only angry at him, but she also couldn't forget the way he'd looked at her when he'd kissed her... as if he actually cared. As if he wanted her the same way he'd wanted her all those years ago. And the ache in her chest, through her body, just wouldn't shift.

Too soon man and dog were back in front of her, making a fuss of each other and of her. Alex smiled again and it did something to her tummy. It felt as if he was trying to break through her defences by smiling that beautiful, sexy 'I want to kiss you again' smile. It wasn't going to work.

It. Would. Not. Work.

He leaned casually on the reception desk, opposite her. 'Did the new doctor and his daughter come in today?'

Beth stood and slapped Button's lead into his hand. 'Yes.'

'They have a dog.'

'Yes.'

She sat down and stared at the desk, noticing the air around her still, and she knew he was looking at her. Waiting. She didn't, couldn't look at him because she was barely holding onto her self-control. That kiss had muddied everything, because now she was cross and turned on and confused and conflicted.

'Beth, does this have to be so awkward?'

Eventually she gained enough strength to raise her eyes, just enough so she could see the buttons on his coat. She wasn't ready to give him eye contact yet. 'Yes.'

He threw up his hands and let Button run off down the pet-shampoo aisle. 'Can we be civil? Maybe try a little conversation? I recommended that Fraser and his daughter come here. They seem nice, right? I hope so, because I'm going to be working closely with him while Joe is on leave and Jenny's off sick.'

Her mother had always told her that if she didn't have anything nice to say, she shouldn't say anything at all. She kept her mouth shut.

Alex didn't. 'What kind of dog do they have? Maybe we could arrange playdates for Spike. They've just moved up from London, so I thought I'd show them some short walks around the place.'

The elephant in the room was lies and betrayal but he wanted to talk about his new workmate. Okay. She directed her focus back on the monitor. She had no idea what was on the screen but she stared at it anyway as she said, 'They have an Old English sheepdog.'

'Beth, please look at me.'

She didn't want to. Couldn't.

'Please. We need to talk. About everything. About the kiss.'

She closed her eyes and tried not to think about it and how good it had felt.

And she hated the difficult atmosphere and wanted the ache in her chest to go. What would

it hurt to hear him out? What would it hurt to look at him?

She raised her head and caught the full heat of his gaze. It made her feel off balance. More, she saw pain in his face as he shook his head and that hit her hard in the chest. 'You lied to me.'

He shook his head. 'I'm sorry, Beth. I was young and confused. I was trying to do the best thing I could by you.'

'By leaving me out of the most difficult and significant thing in your life?'

'Yes. Absolutely.' His eyes were dark, but determination shone through them.

And that was the thing she couldn't get her head around: he was adamant he'd been right to do it. 'I don't understand. I just don't understand. I've been going through it for the last few days and no... I just would not have done something like that to you.'

'I gave you a future.'

'What does that mean?'

He huffed out a breath, then came round to sit on a chair, facing her. It looked as if he was trying to find the right words, or choosing carefully, at least. 'It was December the eighteenth. I'd found a lump and it was big enough for me to know it needed to be seen as soon as possible. On the morning ward round I spoke to the surgeon I was on rotation with. He called his friend,

a urologist, who said if I could get to his morning outpatients clinic he could see me straight away. It's unheard of, I know, but sometimes, if you're lucky—or unlucky to need it in the first place—things fall into place.'

She wasn't sure where this going and what it had to do with her future, because she felt as if it had been ripped away and she hadn't had a say. 'And there wasn't a five-minute gap where you could have called me?'

'I wasn't thinking straight and my mind was whirling with possibilities—none of them good. I wanted facts before I called anyone and all I could think of was Mikey and how it was going to be for me and how I was going to tell everyone I was going to die.' He took a breath and she could see some of the fear he'd been experiencing in the tightness of his shoulders and the haunted eyes. 'So, I had a consult and ultrasound and CT scan that morning, rushed through because the surgeon agreed it was probably malignant…and he'd had a cancellation that afternoon so could fit me in for surgery. Either that or wait three weeks until after the holidays and New Year.'

'You don't want to wait for something like that.'

Alex shrugged in agreement and turned his head a little as he talked, taking his gaze else-

where—she didn't know where. The past? That hospital? 'It was late afternoon and he was telling me the diagnosis and…prognosis. It wasn't good. The ward had been decorated in Christmas stuff and as the doctor was telling me the diagnosis my eyes drifted to a Nativity in the corner. A man, a woman and a baby. And all I could think of was that that was not going to happen to me. I didn't even know if I was going to make Easter. I couldn't stop thinking about that scene and how we'd shaped our lives to that and how much you wanted it.'

'It wouldn't have mattered to me. I would have stood by you.'

His gaze settled back on her. 'You can say that now, but you don't know how you would have reacted as a twenty-one-year-old. You had a lot of living to do and all those plans.'

Plans she still had. Yes, she wanted a family but so far the chances of that happening were literally zero. Generally, a family didn't happen without a partner or a child, neither of which existed in her life right now. 'Plans can change, though. I like to think I would have stayed with you, whatever happened. I would have fought with you, for you.'

He rubbed his hand over his head. 'And that's the whole point, Beth. I didn't *want* you to, can't you see? I'd watched Mikey fight and die. I watched him give up. I fought and fought on his behalf and it didn't work anyway. I watched him change and I changed along with him. It was hard to see someone you love go through that and then to lose them. You know how it was…'

She remembered the whispered behind-the-door arguments about how to deal with the prognosis. How everyone had a different opinion about keeping hope or being honest and accepting fate, Mikey's folks splitting up for a while because they didn't know how to cope with a child dying. She remembered Alex railing against the boundaries his parents had set for him—coming in late, drinking more, arguing back. The anger-fuelled guilt at not being able to help his cousin in the end. 'Your family did some hard grieving.'

'We didn't know how to cope—there are no lessons on that and everyone reacts differently. After Mikey died, we were all so tired and broken by it and I just couldn't do that to you. Besides, more than anything I didn't want you to see me like that. I didn't want you to make promises that you'd feel compelled to keep even if you changed your mind. I certainly didn't want to offer you a future with me that was either pretty damned short or…infertile. I didn't want you regretting your promises and looking over your shoulder for a different life with the family you'd always craved. You'd spent a lot of your life looking after your mum and I saw how much that took out of you. I didn't want you to see me as the same burden.'

'So, you told your parents to tell me you'd gone travelling.' That explained the rush for them to get the suitcases in the car and the guilt that had been written over their faces. And the worry, now she knew why they had been so anxious to get away.

'It had to be something definitive and final so you wouldn't be able to find me and see what was happening. Even though they didn't want to lie they had to do what I asked. They needed me to concentrate on fighting and getting better... if that was possible. Remember, in those first few days we didn't know how long I had. It had spread.' It looked as if it was breaking his heart to tell her this. She slid her hand over to his and squeezed tight. It didn't feel like nearly enough and, more than anything, she wished she'd been with him at the time.

'I'm so sorry. You must have been so scared.' It was devastating to hear this but, even so, she couldn't let him off the hook. 'But what does it say about our relationship that you couldn't share this with me?'

'It says I loved you.' His eyes burnt hot and he looked at her with such affection that she couldn't stop the surge of emotion rising through

her. She was briefly tempted to cover his mouth
with hers and kiss away the pain she knew he
must have had. But there, hammering hard in her
head, was the fact that he'd already broken her
heart once and she couldn't let it happen again.

She slipped her hand out from his and sat
back. 'Weird. Because I always thought that love
meant sticking together through thick and thin.'

'You were twenty-one years old, for God's
sake... No one needs to care for their lover like
that at twenty-one. And...there was a very high
possibility that I wouldn't come out of it down
the track and that you wouldn't get the family
you wanted or even the man you'd fallen for.'

'Wasn't that something I should have decided?
I am so bloody angry with you. You didn't give
me a choice.'

'I was trying to protect you. Protect us both
from a whole lot of heartache.'

'How's that working out for you?' Because
her heart felt as if it had been blown wide open.

His eyebrows peaked. 'I've had better days.
And worse, to be honest. A lot worse.'

She imagined him at twenty-three years of
age, so young and yet sick in hospital, staring at
a possibly bleak future or no future at all, with
no girlfriend to comfort him. And her heart contracted around a hot fist of hurt, regret and sad-

ness. 'Alex, this is madness. I don't know what to say.'

'I had to let you go. I wanted you to have the future you'd always planned for.'

'Without you? We were together for six years. We were engaged to be married. You couldn't trust me with this?'

He huffed out a hollow sound. 'I couldn't bear for you to look at me, at what I was going to become and what I was going to lose. And I knew you'd still want to honour your commitments regardless of how things changed. A pity marriage, Beth? That wasn't what I wanted for either of us.'

'Pity?' That was the furthest from her mind. 'I would never pity you. I loved you.' Her heart squeezed with a too-familiar ache.

Alex's eyes shuttered closed for a moment. When he opened them the irises were black. 'You are loyal and loving and have a beautiful soul, Beth. You would have followed through on your promises no matter what. No matter the consequences to you…or me.'

'I thought we were each other's rocks—through thick and thin—and yet you snatched all that away from me. You didn't give me a chance to care for you. *Care* for you, Alex, care about you. Not pity you. There is a difference.' Her throat was raw with the sting of unshed tears. 'I don't believe this. I thought I knew you as well as I knew myself. We were Alex and Beth for so long it took me years to learn how to be just Beth.'

'You could never be *just* Beth.' He leaned closer and for a moment she wondered if he was going to put his arms around her and whether she would let him. Whether they could possibly develop anything—even friendship—after this. But he just shook his head. 'Don't ever think that. You're amazing. Beautiful. Funny. Sexy. That's why I said I wished things could have been different.'

'So why didn't you come looking for me once you'd finished your treatment? Why didn't you come and tell me what you'd been through? That you were okay and…' *That you wanted me back?* Suddenly the image of a future with him—the same image she'd designed years ago—started to form in her head. He still cared for her, she knew. 'Why wait eight years to come clean about it?'

'Because, in the end, I still can't offer you any future.'

'But you said you got the all-clear.'

He held up his palm again and the look on his face told her that he was not travelling along the same idea path she was. 'You won't get your two point four plus a dog with me. I can't have kids, Beth. Okay?'

'But—'

The door rattled open and she realised she'd forgotten to lock it or put the closed sign up. Alex did that to her: made her forget things and flustered her. But, once upon a time, he'd made her spirits soar too.

He was infertile.

No kids. No family.

She hadn't even thought through the ramifications of his treatment. She hadn't even wondered whether he still wanted the same things. Because she knew damned well that she still did. She hadn't thought past a delicious kiss and this...this mess of lies and some sort of weird idea of protecting her. His weird idea of what love meant.

Dennis Blakely stormed through the door cradling a dog, a beautiful but very sick-looking golden retriever. He was breathing heavily and panic flickered across his face. 'Beth. Beth, can you help?'

She glanced over at Alex. The conversation was over. She had to think and digest what he'd told her and work out what to do next. If anything. But not now.

She ran over to Dennis. There was no blood, no obvious injury to either of them. 'Who is this? What's happened?'

'It's Frank Entwhistle's dog, Alfie. I found him on my farm.'

'What's wrong with him? Bring him through.'

She nodded goodbye to Alex and gave Button a quick stroke then bustled through into the treatment room.

He laid the panting dog onto the examination table. 'Same thing as Meg. Vomiting.'

'Okay.' If it was the same symptoms she knew exactly what the treatment would be, but she couldn't assume anything. 'Why was he at your place?'

'Frank's a stickler for keeping him up at his farm, but he's still in hospital and his family aren't always so careful. My Juney's on heat and I think Alfie's keen. Was keen. He must have got loose and run over the fields.'

Alfie wasn't quite as lethargic and exhausted as Meg had been so chances were he hadn't ingested as much as she had. *If* that was the cause. She couldn't jump to any conclusions despite what her gut instinct was telling her. 'Did you see him eat anything?'

Dennis's back was turned but she saw the lift of his shoulder as she felt Alfie's abdomen. 'No.'

'And June and Meg are fine?'

'Meg's quiet.'

'That's as expected. She's been through a harrowing experience. And your other dog?'

'June's flighty. Same as always.'

'But okay?'

He nodded. No sound.

Beth put Alfie in a holding cage until she'd finished with Dennis. From past experience she knew he'd want to watch over her shoulder so the only way she was going to get him out from under her feet was by walking him out. 'Right, I'll do an examination. You know how it goes… I'll do my best here, Dennis. Go on home and I'll call you when I know more. Can you call Mrs Entwhistle and let her know her boy is here? Thank goodness you acted so quickly.'

His eyes glittered. 'Aye.'

She ushered Dennis out into the reception area and found Alex and Button waiting for her. Alex jumped up from his seat as soon as he saw her. 'Are you okay? Do you need a hand?'

'I thought you'd gone.' She wasn't sure how to talk to him now. The last few days had been beyond intense. 'I can manage. You need to take Button home. It's getting late and he needs his sleep. Routine works best for babies.'

But Alex shook his head, resolute. 'We're staying. If this is anything like Meg you're going to be up all night. I'm not going to let you do that on your own this time. We're not going to let you, are we, Spike?'

'I don't think that's a good idea.'

'We won't get in the way. We'll wait in the staff room, hot drinks at the ready. When you need one just pop your head in.'

It was a kind gesture but she needed space, not an entourage of helpers getting under her feet and wheedling their way further in her heart.

'I don't want you to stay. I can't deal with this right now, Alex. I need time to think.' And breathe and do all those mindless chores that would help settle her head and her heart. She glanced over to Dennis and wondered what he was making of all this, and decided she didn't care right now. She bent and gave her beautiful puppy a good rub then stood to face Alex again. He was looking as if he wanted a good rub too. 'And actually Angus is on call tonight, not me. He'll be back in a few minutes. I'm just covering for him while he does a house call. So, thanks, but I won't be needing you.'

If Alex was stung by her manner he didn't show it. He just nodded. 'Okay. As long as you're okay. We'll talk tomorrow.'

She wanted to say no and that she never wanted to see him again because the more he talked the chasm between them grew.

And she wanted to say yes, because the thought of never seeing him felt like a wound deep in her soul that would never heal.

CHAPTER EIGHT

'So that's the last of it. All boxed up ready for the removals men tomorrow.' Beth stepped back and ignored the catch in her throat. All that was left of her home was a huge pile of boxes, one comfortable chair in the lounge and a large stack of full black bin bags ready to be thrown out. Upstairs, in the room that had been her bedroom sanctuary on and off for nearly thirty years, was just her bed and a suitcase of clothes.

'Didn't we do well?' Her mum grinned as she wheeled her chair around the large empty space, looking a little flushed and possibly with slightly more swollen feet than usual. Beth made a mental note to mention that to the rest home manager when she moved her mum into Bay View tomorrow morning. 'You were certainly a woman with a mission tonight, Beth.'

'Tomorrow's deadline kept me focused.' Amazing what a good dose of anger could do. She'd attacked the last of their possessions in a frenzy, trying to do something to get rid of the ache in her chest. Decluttering had helped a bit but the reason for the decluttering had shifted the ache sideways, infusing it with sadness that her mum had become debilitated enough to need daily care. But she tried to be cheerful for her mum's sake. 'The truck will be here at eight, so we need to be up early.'

'I'll set an alarm.'

'I won't need one. I'm bound to be awake.' Sleep had been pretty elusive ever since she'd kissed Alex. Of course, she couldn't tell her mum that was the reason. 'I'm probably going to be worrying about the golden retriever that Angus is looking after tonight. He was pretty sick.'

'You overthink, you always have. Let Angus do the worrying. And thank him for letting you have the day off to help me move.'

'Hey, I'm just the locum helping him out for a few weeks. He owes me for taking the pressure off at a busy time of year.' Beth bent down and wrote on the box lids with a thick black Sharpie.

Kitchen Glasgow
Lounge Glasgow
Photos Bay View
Bedroom Glasgow
Lounge Glasgow 2

Okay, so she'd clearly agreed to keep more than she'd intended, but at least her mum was sorted. 'I'm so happy you're looking forward to moving into your new place.'

'Change can be good. I'm going to make sure it is. Oh, I left the little Christmas tree out for you. I thought you could dress it. Something to make the place look festive until you leave.'

'I thought you were going to take it with you for your room.' Beth looked over at the three-feet-tall Christmas tree on the floor next to the boxes. 'I'm not much in the mood for a tree.'

Her mum wheeled over and, wincing with pain at even the slightest movement, picked it up and straightened out the branches. 'You should make an effort, Beth. It will make you feel good to see the glitter and the trimmings. Christmas is a funny time of year... There's always so much anticipation. But I've had good ones, bad ones, boring ones, funny ones, ones where the turkey was off and we ended up opening a tin of corned beef...'

Rocking back on her heels Beth joined her mum in the trip down Memory Lane. They'd been doing that a lot recently. 'I remember that one. It didn't seem to matter what we ate in the end—we had fun anyway.'

'Exactly. It was the company that made it special. That first Christmas with you. Oh, my.

That was the very best. Always.' Her mum's eyes filled with tears and, unlike Beth, who tried hard never to be seen crying, she let them fall. 'The first one without your dad. That was hard.'

So shocked by her father's sudden death, Beth could hardly remember a Christmas celebration even happening that year. 'Did we go to Aunty Jackie's in Leicester?'

Her mum nodded and swiped at her cheek with her cardigan sleeve. 'And she got drunk and ended up shouting at the Queen when she was doing her speech. Every Christmas is different, Beth, that's what I'm saying. In the end it's what you make it. I have no idea what it's going to be like in Bay View, but I have no doubt we'll all try to have fun.'

'They seemed a lively bunch when we went to the viewing. Are you sure you're okay about going? Really, really sure?'

'Darling, I never wanted to move from here, and you know that. This has been my home for thirty-five years. It was a huge admission that I couldn't cope any more, and it took me a long time to be okay with it, but sometimes you have to pull on your big girl's panties and get on with it. Like you giving Alex a chance to be your friend or at least get some peace with what happened.'

She hadn't mentioned the kiss, but while doing

the packing Beth had told her mum about what had happened to Alex and between them they'd tried to make sense of it.

'There's a lot of water under the bridge… many, many years. You don't want to be carrying all that hurt around with you and letting it give you sleepless nights.' She gave Beth the kind of knowing look only a mother could give. 'You're grown-ups now, you're different people from who you were a decade ago.'

'I had got over him, until…' the kiss '…until he told me the truth. I just can't get over the fact he lied to me.'

The anger she'd worn as a badge and a barrier had been cracked open by that kiss. He'd thought letting her go was a gift. He'd broken things off because he'd thought that was best for her and not for him. It was cockeyed logic, but she could see how, in extremis, you might turn your thoughts inside out. If he really did believe he'd been doing the right thing she couldn't hold that against him, could she? But she was bruised that his parents had been complicit in keeping it from her. She hadn't just lost her boyfriend, but also the family she'd come to love and see as her own.

'He might not have handled things the way you would have, but he did it with a good heart. He is a good man, Beth.' Her mum straightened the tree branches out, fluffing up the green strands that hung sadly as if empathising with Beth's mood. 'Obviously I knew him as a young adult who loved you so much, and then when he came back to take over his father's place at the practice a couple of years ago I saw how good he is with the patients and the staff. He's always willing to listen and help. He even did a house call on Dennis Blakely, and, trust me, only a saint would do that. And he's kind. Look at how he's taking care of that dog. I just think you should listen to what he has to say.'

Which wasn't helping Beth at all, because she preferred being spectacularly cross…that way she didn't have to acknowledge the other feelings swirling in her gut. The ones that took notice of the way he'd offered to help her with Alfie and the way he'd kept on talking about anything and everything just to break down the barriers she'd built. The way he'd kissed her.

Oh, that kiss.

'And I wanted to tell you one more thing, Elizabeth Grace Masters.'

'Oh-oh. Full name.' She smiled up at her mum while guilt wriggled through her. Parents could do that to you. It was the same kind of feeling Beth got when she was pulled over for a routine police check. 'What have I done now?'

But her mum was beaming. 'Amazing things.

Selfless and wonderful things. You were eight
when I was diagnosed with this horrible disease
and with every flare-up you slipped into being
my carer with no complaint. Ever. You were always there for me.'

'Not true. I went to university.'

'Only because I made you go.'

And if she hadn't Beth wouldn't have the qual-
ifications and experience she had now. An ease
to be able to do the job anywhere. The opportunity to make a difference to the lives of, not just
animals, but their humans too. But she'd give it
all up in a heartbeat if it meant her mum could
be pain-free and reclaim some of her independ-
ence. 'You know I'd do it all again.'

'I know you would. But now I'm going to have
help twenty-four-seven, so when you come down
we can do nice things instead of you always having to do boring chores for me. And you need
to put yourself first. Let your hair down. Take
chances that are offered to you without thinking about me.'

'Ha! Chances? In Oakdale?'

'Anywhere you want to go, my girl. Glasgow.
South America. Asia. Or yes, right here in Oakdale.'

The way she was feeling about being around
Alex, the moon wouldn't be enough distance away.

Her mum put the tree on the floor and reached

out for a hug. Beth went into her arms the way she'd been doing since she was a little girl. 'I love you, Mum.'

'I love you too, Elizabeth Grace.' There was a little wobble in her voice. 'Right, grab the wine. Put some music on. Let's get the tree decorated.'

It was surely one of the scrappiest trees ever made and, as it had sat on Beth's drawers in her bedroom every Christmas for over two decades, it was a little battered and worn. It should probably have been put in the bin bags along with the other rubbish, but her mum wanted to do this and she had no real excuse as to why not. Plus, it wouldn't take long to hang half a dozen baubles on it anyway.

She rooted in the box marked *Xmas Decs*. The first bauble was one her grandmother had given her when she was a toddler, a wooden reindeer with red antlers. As she hung it up she remembered her grandma's smile and the lovely hugs she used to give. With the next bauble she remembered her dad, and the way his Christmas hat always fell over his eyes just as he was about to carve the turkey, and she'd laugh so hard and tug it up so she could see his dancing eyes. And then, Aunty Jackie singing karaoke. Badly.

Beth was surprised to notice her chest wasn't quite as tight as she hung bauble after bauble on the tree. She even managed a smile as she found the sparkly angel Alex had bought her one year. She'd been so happy then and, yes, she could be again. Geez, she had been happy many times in the last few years without him.

So, her mum was right, each Christmas was different and it was up to her to make them the best they could be. This year Beth would be sitting with her mum, sharing food with a bunch of lovely people. Who knew where she'd be next year and who she'd be spending it with? She could look at that as a challenge or as an exciting secret yet to be unwrapped. Anyone would choose the unwrapped secret, right?

And if she was capable of thinking happy thoughts about next year, then she could think happy thoughts about now. Her mum was going to be cared for so that was one less worry. She had a job in Glasgow and a house she loved. She'd reacquainted with Alex and even managed conversations. He'd told her about his darkest times and she'd looked at it all from her point of view and not his. So, if she truly had loved him, she could at least wonder how it had been for him, if nothing else. She could be kind and compassionate—all the things she was in her job and to everyone else. She could listen to the man who had once been her whole world.

Listen. That was all. Because she couldn't trust herself, or him, to do the kissing thing again. That was a step further than she was ready to take.

By the time they'd finished hanging the baubles she had a little warm glow. She stood up and stretched, glancing round at what else needed doing before bed. 'I'll just put these bags in the rubbish bin outside.'

Her mum nodded. 'Then we can watch the last of the tidying programmes on my tablet.'

'I'm not sure we need to watch them any more. Our job here is done. We are the declutter queens.' Although Beth still hadn't found the right place to put her emotions.

Her mum looked at the bags that numbered almost as many as the boxes. 'Are you sure you want to throw so much out?'

'Fresh start. For both of us, right?' Beth hauled the bags up and shuffled out to the front door.

The night sky was bright with diamond stars and the air was crisp and fresh. There wasn't a sound, and with the icy white blanket over the roofs and paths and the little strings of lights crisscrossing the village square it looked quite magical, like a scene from a children's Christmas book. She stopped to lean on the gate, half expecting Santa Claus and his sleigh to appear out of the sky, the way she'd wished he had and dreamt he would for so many years growing up.

This house, this view, this garden had been

her safety net. This home with her mum, that she'd come back and forth to over the years, had always been here for her. In a week or so she'd hand in the keys and go back to Glasgow. It was as if she was closing a door on her past. She breathed deeply. Yes, that was what she needed to do. Close the door and start looking forward again.

She was just shutting the gate when she heard a man's voice. She turned quickly to her left and there he was.

Alex. *Of course.* Out walking Button, their backs to her as they meandered down the street. Their footprints were in the snow right in front of her…shoes and paws in a scudded mush of slush. And she wondered if they'd paused when they got here, or hurried past. Whether Button had caught her scent and sniffed and whether Alex had thought about her, about them. About where to next.

She considered calling to them, but instead watched for a moment as they waded through the snow side by side, his long legs making easy strides and the quick hop-bounce of Button's baby steps. Then the pup abruptly stopped. As dogs did. To sniff or wee or chew on something. She smiled to herself as Alex gently tugged on the lead and Button kept right on sniffing. He tugged again and Button took no notice. Eventually, Alex crouched, tickled the dog's neck and said something she couldn't hear.

And as she watched she absent-mindedly scooped up some snow from the garden wall and ran it through her fingers. Damn, it was the kind of cold that burned. The kind of snow that made perfect snowballs.

She ran her palm along the wall and scooped up more snow. Crushed it into a ball. And she watched Alex, crouched to the dog, and her heart did a little wobble. She tried to tell herself it was because she'd become too attached to the puppy and she was going to have to leave it behind when she left, but it was more than that.

It was Alex. Why did everything have to be so confusing? She'd come here with a clear vision and things had got messy in her heart and her head. Even when she reaffirmed her purpose he was still there, muddying everything. Why did Alex make her feel so much?

What she needed was something to get all this pent-up emotion out of her system. Sex? Not a good idea because the only man she could imagine having sex with was Alex and that was simply out of the question. Getting drunk? Perhaps. But she only had a half-bottle and she was going to share that with her mum. She compacted the snow in her hand. The perfect snowball.

Oh. She smiled to herself. Here was just the thing.

Target practice.

Alex took a deep breath and let it out slowly, watching his breath curl into the air and then fade away, and wondered what he'd done to deserve a puppy who took absolutely no notice of him and yet seemed to snap to attention whenever Beth was around.

Beth. Yeah. That last conversation hadn't gone as well as he'd hoped, but his cards were on the table now.

'I did the right thing, Spike. I've finally been completely honest and I feel just a bit more… freed up.' He was talking to the dog as if it was his confidant. Go figure. But, judging by the way Spike was sniffing at the electricity pole, he had a feeling this man's best friend wasn't listening. Something had caught his attention. Probably something dead. But the dog wouldn't budge so Alex had bent down to see what, if anything, was so interesting. Nothing. Just snow and stones. 'She won't want to love me now, so that's good. There won't be any more confusion or unnecessary emotion.' Just a few more days until she left. He could deal with that. He could deal with being close to her if he knew she wasn't going to be here for ever.

If she was going to stay here for ever then he'd have to move somewhere far away; he had a feeling the moon wouldn't be far enough. Spike gave him a big lick on his cheek then bounded away, the lead dragging behind him making a little trail in the snow.

'Hey! Spike! Come ba—' As he straightened and started to turn round to see where Spike had run off to something hard thudded against his shoulder. What the—? Clumps of snow fell from his coat. A snowball?

He whipped round and saw Beth leaning on her gate, fist in the air. *Gotcha!*

Spike at her feet.

She looked victorious and animated and breathtaking and was already patting snow in her hands for another snowball shot. He walked directly into the line of fire, chancing that she wouldn't throw if he was actually walking towards her. 'Hey, crazy girl, you could have hit my puppy.'

Crazy girl. She wasn't the girl he'd fallen in love with back in his teens, she was a stunning, independent, staggeringly beautiful woman and, even if he hadn't been mad about her a decade ago, nothing could have stopped him from being attracted to who she was now.

She smiled, and it was the first time in days that he'd seen it. 'Not a chance. I'm not that bad at throwing and do you honestly think I would have missed you? I've been sharpening my skills for long enough.'

At least she was talking. 'Truce?'

'Tempting, but no.' She stuffed more snow into his neck and the ice slithered down his spine. Cold, but not cold enough to douse the need building inside him. He'd closed himself off from wanting anyone for years, but she made him want. She made him hot. She made him need. She made him wish for things out of reach. And yet he kept on wanting them.

'Right. You asked for it.' He scooped snow into his palm and rubbed it on her neck, making her scream. She squirmed and turned into him, so close her scent was in the air, making him inhale sharply—he just couldn't get enough—and wish he were buried deep inside her.

'Okay, truce! Alex. Truce.'

'Don't like your own medicine, eh?' He bent and clipped Spike's lead onto his collar and lifted him up to see her. 'Spike says hi and please don't throw snowballs at my nice daddy.'

'Hello, lovely boy. By which I mean the dog. Obviously.' As she fussed over Spike her eyes were shining and she seemed brighter, happier, more relaxed than she'd been before. 'And hello, Alex.'

Still, he stuck to safe subjects. 'How's Alfie? Have you heard?'

She wiped her hand over her forehead, missing a bit of snow that was stuck to her hair, but he let it be and let her talk. 'I got a call from Angus an hour or so ago. He's pretty sure Alfie has ingested something. It's not a systemic illness, there's no temperature, no obvious disease process. An acutely inflamed gut. An unhappy dog. Not as ill as Meg, but enough to be kept in overnight.'

'So, whatever it was, he's eaten the same thing? Is that what you think?' Spike was chewing Alex's coat sleeve. 'Spike! Stop that.'

'He's bored. Puppies chew when they're teething too, so it could be that. Put him on the ground and let him have a sniff around.'

'He probably needs to walk. As do I. My feet are getting numb.' He stamped his feet as Spike pawed at Beth's leg. 'And he wants you to come too.'

A corner of her mouth lifted. 'I said I'd sit with Mum. It's her last night with me. She's going to Bay View tomorrow.'

Of course. 'Totally get it. No worries.'

'Okay, I'll see you in the morning for handover.'

'Sure.'

She turned and clicked the waist-high gate behind her but stopped. Then she looked back at him. 'Actually, I do need to talk to you quickly about something.'

'I'm all ears.' His heart spasmed. Whatever she wanted to say, he'd listen. He'd take on board what she thought, because, even though he still totally believed he'd done the right thing, he could see how badly he'd hurt her in the process.

'About Alfie and Meg and Dennis… I just need to talk things through…you know, theories, ideas…possible causes…' she clarified.

Right. Not everything was about him. She'd made that very clear more than once. 'Sure. Of course. Now? Or tomorrow?'

'I don't…' She frowned and gave a little shrug. 'It's just a feeling I've got. It's probably nothing.'

'Or…? Maybe it's something. Can it wait?'

She pursed her lips, breathed out. 'You know, no. I want to talk it through with you and morning handovers are always busy, especially tomorrow as I'm going to drop Button with the team at the clinic for the morning and then take Mum to Bay View. So… I'll just grab my coat and let my mum know I'm walking with my boy for a few minutes.' She kissed Spike. 'That is still you. Still not Alex.'

'Hey, I'm getting the message, loud and clear.'

Within minutes she came running out, a turquoise puffer jacket billowing behind her as she shoved her arms into the sleeves. They headed out on the path up towards Oak's Top, a little hill of oak trees that gave the village its name.

And as they trudged she talked. 'So, I'm thinking that if both dogs have eaten something we need to find out what it is before any other pooch gets hurt. It's a puzzle. I was sure Meg had ingested some tablets she shouldn't have got into, but how could Alfie have eaten the same thing?'

'Unless it's a plant or something they're attracted to. Or something to do with things they use on the farm, perhaps? Fertiliser or insecticide?'

'Everything's covered in snow and I'm pretty certain they don't use those sprays until spring. I'm not sure there'd be anything for them to get at. What else could it be? Not chocolate—you see that in the stuff they bring up. Maybe it's antifreeze. It's sweet and dogs like to drink it. Maybe one of Dennis's trucks is leaking, or he's being careless with the bottles and leaving them around the farm where the dogs can get into them.'

'Maybe.'

'Could be Dennis's water supply?'

'He's okay though.'

'It's likely not the water. I'm going to have to have another think.' She sighed. 'Have you heard anything about Frank?'

'He's sore but off the critical list. They removed his spleen and his liver was badly bruised along with three broken ribs, but he'll be okay. Lesson learnt, Beth, keep away from tupped-out rams.'

'I'll bear that in mind.' She grinned at him. 'But here's something else. When I went back through June's notes I found that she's been in with a series of weird symptoms too—she saw the previous clinic owner a couple of times and then the locums. Angus has had two different locums. Dennis also brought in a cat that he said had been staggering and acting strangely but on examination they found nothing of any consequence. So, he's brought in four pets with similar symptoms, seen by four different vets.'

'That's the problem with having locums. They don't see patterns of behaviour.' Something previously fractured and blurred started to take shape in his head. 'Patterns of *owner* behaviour. Do you think...' the notion that someone could hurt their own pet was so troubling he was starting to doubt himself '...it's some sort of attention-seeking thing?'

Her eyebrows rose. 'He's been reporting symptoms no one else could see.'

'Until now. Meg was really sick. Alfie too.' He didn't want the piece of the jigsaw to fit. 'Do you think...? No. No.'

'What?'

He felt sick. 'That Dennis is doing it? Making them ill and then bringing them in? Escalating the urgency with poisoning?'

'No. Why would he do that? He wouldn't, would he?' She shook her head, her eyes widening as she thought more. 'It must be accidental. It's more likely he's forgetting things or misplacing them. You know, like people with early dementia. Unless…unless he's having some sort of breakdown.'

'In either case he needs help. Urgent help.' Alex looked at his watch. It was late and this kind of thing needed to be dealt with carefully. Turning up in the thick of night would only put Dennis on the back foot. And it was all just a whole load of supposition and ideas with nothing substantial to tie them together. 'I'll go to see him tomorrow.'

She stopped walking and put her hand on his arm, genuine concern in her eyes. 'Are you sure?'

'Of course. We need to get to the bottom of this.'

'You shouldn't go on your own. Take someone…the new guy? What's-his-name? Fraser?'

'He's got a Well Child clinic all morning, then a training thing in the afternoon. Besides, it's not exactly the best kind of welcome, is it? Can you come and help me suss out whether a patient is hurting his animals?' It was an improbable idea.

They were still climbing the hill and her breath came fast, puffing little whorls of steam into the air. 'What about Joe? Could he go with you?'

'He's on leave with his family and I'm not going to bother him with this. I'm booked up all day, but I can scoot up there on my lunch break.'

She nodded, resolute. 'I'll go with you. I should be done with moving Mum by then and she'll be wanting her afternoon nap.'

'Are you sure?'

'Absolutely, this is my case, these are my clients. I'll come with you.'

He reminded himself she was leaving; that was the only way he could convince himself to keep away. 'How's the packing going?'

Trudging through the snow was hard work, and she had a sheen of moisture on her forehead. She wiped it away with the back of her hand. 'Finished. In the nick of time. The removals people are coming early and I'm going to drive Mum over and get her settled. She's at that point where she just wants it to happen.'

'How do you feel about it now?'

Her nose crinkled as she grimaced. 'Oh, you know, weird. Happy that she's found somewhere she likes, but a bit strange that I won't have a home to come back to any weekend I want to see her.'

'You could stay with me.' The words blabbed out before he could stop them.

She blinked and looked at him with a zillion questions in her eyes. And a very definite no.

He corrected himself. 'Just offering, as a friend. I have plenty of rooms. Too many.'

Rooms she'd have filled with kids and animals. Rooms that were now empty spaces.

They were at the top of the hill now, looking down at the village below. It had been their favourite walk when they were younger, and he wondered whether she was thinking that too. In winter they'd drag toboggans up here, in summer they'd lain in the long grass and whispered promises to each other in between kisses. He wondered if she remembered, if she was thinking the same things, and whether she was wanting to revisit those kisses the same way he ached to.

Because no matter how much he told himself to rewire and stop wanting her, it wasn't happening. He still wanted her. He tried rewiring again. She was leaving. He'd have to get used to being here without her again. 'And then…you'll be going back to Glasgow.'

'Going home, yes. What should we do about Button? No one's come forward to claim him and he's getting more and more attached to us.' She didn't add that it worked the other way too but Alex had to admit he was likely to miss the little terror once he was gone to his new family... whoever that was. She bent and gave the puppy a stroke. 'I'm leaving in a few days and there's no way he can stay at mine. I'm sole charge of the clinic, it's too busy and I have no home back up.'

'Likewise. I'm not sole charge now, but my life isn't geared to a dog. I work long hours and he'd get bored at home on his own. It's just not fair on a lively puppy.'

'What will we do?'

'I've put adverts everywhere. Someone's bound to reply soon. We'll have to make sure whoever has him knows what they're doing. I don't want him going to just anyone.'

Her eyes grew big and she laughed. 'Someone who has no idea how to look after a puppy would be terrible, right?'

'You talking about me?'

'Of course. But I have to say you're a fast learner, and not everyone would be willing to house a boisterous puppy.'

'He has his uses.' Like, an excuse to come walking. Like, a reason for him to meet up with Beth twice a day. Spike had been the best way of breaching the yawning gap...even if it had meant a sad goodbye to his best climbing shoes.

'He makes for a good hot-water bottle,' he explained, quickly.

'Do not tell me you still let him sleep with you?'

'There's no one else there to mind. What's the harm?'

'Alex Norton, if I was sharing your bed I'd mind a lot if there was a puppy there too. Oh. I didn't mean…' Even in the dark he saw the heat in her eyes and the bloom on her cheeks. 'Oh, you know what I mean. I wasn't talking about us.'

'I know. Beth, I know.' But the thought was there. The temptation to pull her to him and kiss her senseless was almost overwhelming. Because this was perfect. This. The three of them, here at the top of the hill, the clear black sky, the promise of snow. The silence filled only by them. It was like it had been years ago and yet, different. Because they were both different now. And he wondered how things might have been before his body had let him down and pulled his dreams down with it.

Could he reach to her? One more time?

But she turned away and wrapped her arms around her chest. 'Come on, let's get home. I'm freezing to death. And Mum's going to wonder where I've got to.'

And just like that the moment was gone, along with his chance.

CHAPTER NINE

BETH TRIED TO focus on her mum all morning but sometimes—like now, as her mum made the life-affirming decision as to which drawer to put her nightwear in, and then perfected the folding technique they'd seen on TV—her thoughts drifted.

Could it be possible that Dennis was knowingly giving contaminated food to the dogs?

No. No, she wouldn't entertain that thought. But even so, going up to Oaktree Farm to play detective made her a little uneasy. Not physically, not at all, but she wasn't confident at dealing with confused or defensive patients. She was glad she'd have Alex with her. Safety in numbers would be best.

Her heart gave a little jump at the thought of him. And she had to admit that last night had been a step in the right direction. Being on Oak's Top had felt right. Until she'd almost suggested that sharing his bed might happen, or be a good thing or…

She checked her watch. Twelve fifteen. He should have called her by now. His afternoon clinic started at two, so he was fast running out of time to get up to Dennis's and back. She called the clinic and, after lengthy 'How are you?'s back and forth with Maxine, she was put through. 'Did you forget we were going up to see Dennis?'

'I'm sorry. One of the Archer kids is having a serious asthma attack and I'm waiting for the ambulance. I can't leave, not yet.'

'No, of course not. Stay there.' There was no choice. He was the doctor; she was the vet. 'I have to pick up Button from the clinic. I can't take advantage of their generosity any longer. I said I'd be there at twelve and it's now almost twenty past and I haven't left yet. I'll get him and then I'll go see Dennis.'

'No. Absolutely not. I don't want you going on your own. We'll go together, later.'

His voice was firm and commanding, and for a millisecond she thought about agreeing. But she couldn't wait. Who knew how long Alex was going to be dealing with a sick child? And if Dennis really was hurting his animals, he needed to be stopped.

It was a slithery, slippery journey up an icy road flanked by oaks and too many times she skidded. But finally up at Oaktree Farm Beth parked in the courtyard, took a big deep breath and climbed out.

'Stay here, Button. I won't be long.' She left a window slightly open, a blanket in case he got cold and a bowl of water on the floor of the car, then walked across the courtyard.

On her right the barn doors had been drawn open and there were fresh tyre tracks in the snow. If he wasn't here then he was out, somewhere, on his farm. God knew where.

Maybe he'd been out and returned already. She hammered on the door. No answer. She pushed it open and called again, 'Dennis! It's me, Beth, from the vet's.'

There was a bowl of fresh dog food on the floor by the front door. She looked closely and it all looked normal but…wait. Was that powder in there? Or snow? Or was it her imagination conjuring things up? Not quite believing she was doing this, she scooped some of the food into a plastic bag and stuffed it into her handbag. She'd send that off for analysis when she got back to the clinic. As she straightened a collie appeared from a room further in the house.

'Are you June?' The dog looked up at her then whined and came slowly over to sniff Beth's hand. 'Are you okay, girl? Where's Dennis? Dennis? Dennis?'

But the dog just lay down on the hall floor.

'What's the matter, old girl?' She stroked the dog's head and bent to take a better look at her when she was barrelled from behind, almost toppling over.

It was Meg, barking and rubbing her nose into Meg's hip.

'Hey, Meg. Hey, girl. How're you doing?'

The dog looked as if she'd recovered from her ordeal. She let Beth fuss her and check she was okay and then ran outside. And back inside again. Beth breathed out. The old mutt had got her energy back at least. Meg ran to the door and stopped, looking back at Beth. Then bounded over and tugged on her coat. Then back to the door.

'Where's Dennis?' Beth asked as Meg ran back and forth, barking. 'Do you want me to come with you?'

What to do? June looked exhausted and melancholy and there was definitely something not right with her. *Thank God I left Button in the car.*

Meg nuzzled against Beth's leg then sank her teeth into Beth's coat and tugged. 'You want me to come with you? Is…is it Dennis? Where is he?'

Something skittered down her spine. Ice. Fear. Meg was running in circles, frantic…to the door, to Beth, to the door, to Beth.

It was eerily quiet. Where was Dennis? She

looked at her phone. The reception signal bars dipped and then rose and then disappeared altogether. Further down the hall she found an ancient landline and picked up the receiver. No dial tone. Damn. It had been working the other day when she rang him. Maybe the recent heavy snow had brought the lines down?

She tried to control her panicky heart as she thought. She couldn't call Alex to discuss what she should do. She was on her own. Did she bundle June into the car and take her to the clinic? Did she go with Meg to find Dennis? And why was Meg so frantic? That was not a good sign. Meg? June? Or Dennis?

The lethargic collie was at least safe and warm in the house and wasn't having seizures and there was no sign of vomiting. And Meg was frantic. She made her decision. 'Okay, girl. Show me.'

After shoving the bowl of food outside and then closing the door to make sure June couldn't get to it, Beth followed the collie out to the right of the farm and along tyre tracks that veered off up a hill.

The dog clearly knew exactly where she was going and kept running ahead and then back checking Beth was following. But Beth wasn't as fit or as agile as a collie and the uphill hike whipped the breath from her lungs. It was as if ice hung in the air, thick and heavy, making everything slippery. Up and up they went following fresh thick tracks. A tractor or quad?

They topped the hill and she tracked across the landscape looking for something. She didn't know what. But as she peered down to her left she spied something that jarred. Something red and metal.

She started towards it and as she got closer saw it was a quad bike, tyres uppermost.

'Oh, my God, he's fallen off the quad.' She started to run but it was too hard to maintain a grip and the next thing she knew she was tumbling over and over down the hill, ricocheting off small stones and rocks, wincing at pain in her shoulder, the small of her back, her left thigh. Eventually she came to a stop face first in the snow and still metres from Dennis. *Damn.*

Her heart thumped hard and she tried to suck frigid air into her lungs. She was here, alone. There was a sick dog back at the farm and Dennis underneath a quad bike. She needed to be calm and not put herself in danger too. Wasn't the first rule of emergency rescue to make sure the rescuer was safe?

Okay. Big breath. And another.

Putting all her weight through her arms, she shoved herself upright, put her foot out and pitched forwards on the ice.

She didn't have time to care as she stumbled

and slid down the hill, placing her feet in the tyre grooves in the snow to give her boot tread something to grip on. She was tired and aching and breathless when she reached the upturned quad.

Dennis was there, his leg wedged underneath the engine. The snow around his head was a red halo.

Head injury? Leg crushed. She knelt down, ignoring the cold and wet spreading through her jeans and into her bones. She took off her thick jacket and laid it over him in some vain attempt to warm him despite the snow, then investigated the head injury. He had a large gash across the back of his head caused, she imagined, by a jagged rock sticking up through the snow. She gently shook his arm. 'Dennis? Dennis? Can you hear me?'

He didn't move.

Pressing freezing fingers to his neck, she searched for a pulse. 'Come on, Dennis. Please.' *Please.*

There. There it was, faint and thready and slow. He was barely clinging on, but alive. She put her weight against the quad, pushing as hard as she could. But it didn't move. How long had he been here?

She shook him again. Then tapped his cheek. It was like ice, his skin like parchment and his lips a pale blue. 'Dennis. Can you hear me?'

Okay. What to do? With shaking fingers she fumbled for her phone, tried again for a signal. Nothing.

She breathed as slowly as she could and worked through things logically. Unconscious or fast slipping away? 'Dennis, talk to me. Dennis.'

A gurgle came from his throat and his mouth opened a fraction.

'Dennis, it's Beth.' There was no way she was going to be able to lift the quad from his leg, not on her own. She needed help.

She needed Alex.

More than ever, she needed to see him. To see his steady and unshakeable calm. She didn't want to admit it right now, but the thought of him warmed her through. More. The thought of him made her body prickle with heat and longing. But he wasn't here, he was stuck with a sick child back at the village and that was where he should be. Damn. No phone signal. No Alex. She was on her own.

Even if she could get him out from under the quad she wouldn't be able to get him up and over that hill. The only way Dennis had a chance was if she got help. Maybe…maybe there'd be some phone reception on higher ground? Failing that she'd have to get in her car and drive until she got a signal.

'Dennis?' She rubbed his arms and legs in a,

likely vain, attempt to get his circulation going. 'Dennis, I don't know if you can hear me, but it's Beth. I'm here. I'm going to get help. Just hold on for me, please. June and Meg need you to hold on.'

The dog whimpered at her name and she came and licked Dennis's cheek. His eyes flickered open. 'I'm…'

'I'm going to get help, Dennis. Meg's here. Meg, come here.' She got the dog to lie on his chest, hoping she'd infuse warmth into him and a will to survive. 'Stay, Meg. Stay, girl.'

His lips moved again and she leaned close to hear. 'So…sorry…'

'It's okay. I'll get help, Dennis. Please. Meg needs you. June needs you. Hold on.'

Alex pulled into Oaktree Farm courtyard and cranked the handbrake. Beth's car was parked askew. She was here, then, despite the fact he'd told her to wait for him.

He jumped out of the car and looked around. Knocked on the front door. Twice.

'Beth? Dennis? Anyone here?' He pushed the door open and nearly tripped. June was lying on the hall floor and she raised her head as he barrelled in. 'June? Where's Dennis? And Beth?'

But the dog just lay at his feet and whined.

This didn't feel right. He didn't like the whining. He didn't like the silence when the whining stopped. Surely, he should be hearing Beth and Dennis talking? Surely, they'd come to his calls? Where was Meg?

He wandered outside and saw footprints heading off behind the barn so he followed them, his pace fuelled by the uneasy feeling in the pit of his gut.

'Beth? Dennis? Beth?' he called out to the wet blanket of mist that was quickly descending. Damn, it was so cold. How did Dennis live up here? Why? And where the hell were they? Why hadn't she called him? Why hadn't she just damned well waited?

He breached the top of the hill and saw a small figure heading down away from him into the distance, trudging through knee-deep snow. His heart jumped in relief that she was okay, and also in a sudden need to beat to her rhythm. Where was she going? 'Beth? Beth?'

He started to move towards her, but his foot slid on a sheet of ice and his arms cartwheeled to keep his balance. 'Beth!'

She stopped and turned. 'Alex?' Her voice was thin and whipped away by the wind.

But she ran back towards him, stumbling and slipping, reaching to the ground to get purchase through the steeper parts, and he ran towards her, fighting to keep upright and fighting to stop the crazy relief that she was safe overwhelming him and making his steps stutter.

She was breathless, her cheeks pink with exertion, and she looked spooked as they met somewhere halfway. 'Alex. Thank God.'

'What's happened? Where's your jacket? You must be freezing.' He slipped his coat off and put it round her shoulders.

She looked surprised as she slid her arms into his coat sleeves, as if she hadn't realised she wasn't wearing one. 'It's Dennis, he's had an accident on the quad. It's bad. His head's bleeding and his leg is crushed. He has a pulse and he's vaguely conscious, but I'm not hopeful. He's down there, looks like the quad might have skidded or something, anyway it's on top of him and I couldn't get it off.'

As he peered in the direction she was pointing he could see a red stain in the middle of white. From memory the quad was ancient and rusting and probably weighed a whole lot more than she did. 'Call an ambulance.'

'I just did. I had to run to the top of the hill to get phone reception. They're on their way but… oh, Alex.' Her face crumpled and she looked as if she needed a hug. Without thinking he put his arms round her and felt her momentarily sag against him. 'I got Meg to lie gently on him, in a place I didn't think he was injured, so she could keep him warm. I hope that was okay.'

'It's fine, Beth, you've done everything right so far. We'll do what we can to help him.'

It was the first physical contact they'd had since the kiss and he couldn't help notice, through the rush of adrenaline, how perfectly she fitted against him. Her hair was cold against his cheek but he pressed his face into it, just damned glad she was okay. He wanted to kiss away that tension in her body, to comfort her in more ways than this. He wanted her to not have seen what had happened to Dennis. Whatever that was.

She pushed away from him but held his gaze. 'Thank you, I needed that. But come on. Quick.'

The old man was in bad shape. Alex untied his scarf and used it to stem the bleeding from the head wound while he did a quick assessment. 'It's not just the blood loss I'm concerned about, there's hypothermia and the weight of the quad on his leg is compromising his blood supply. Any idea how long he's been out here?'

'No idea.' She shook her head and put her hand over his. 'I'll do this, you look at his leg.'

From what he could see it was a mess, but he couldn't assess the full extent of the damage without lifting the quad off his limb. 'Dennis, can you hear me?'

The old farmer's eyes flickered open, then closed again. Good. A reaction at least.

'I'm going to lift the quad, okay? It's going to hurt but I'm going to be as quick as I can.'

Beth slid her hand into the old man's. 'Dennis, I'm here. Hold my hand. I'm here. Alex is here. He'll get you safe, okay? Just hold on.'

Alex took off his trouser belt and tied it around Dennis's thigh. 'I can see there's a lot of blood loss there too. If I need to I can tighten the belt and stop any more bleeding. I just have to get eyes on the injury asap. I have to move the quad.'

'Okay. Do it.' She looked up at Alex and he felt her trust in him to save this man as a punch to his heart. And also a heavy weight in his chest, because if he didn't raise the quad and save their client he'd have failed her. But he used the force of her trust to power up the strength in his body. He pressed his shoulder against the quad and pushed hard. Pushed again. And with an ominous creak the machine lifted.

Beth inhaled sharply and he could see the grip on her hand tightening. The old man was gripping on.

He couldn't risk aggravating any potential damage Dennis might have done to his back by moving him at all, so somehow he managed to shift the angle of the quad and release it off to the side with a sickening crunch.

Dennis's leg was indeed a mess. 'It's a complicated fracture and I'm worried he's compromised the blood supply to his foot. He needs urgent surgery.' Where the hell was the helicopter?

He tightened the tourniquet and packed ice around the leg. And then the distant whir of blades set off a rush of relief through his veins.

The two paramedics brought pain relief, oxygen and blankets and while they worked on getting Dennis ready to be transferred onto a stretcher Alex handed over. 'His veins are thin and collapsing. We should do an intraosseous infusion in his left leg to get some fluids into him.'

The lead paramedic nodded. 'I'll give you a hand with that and Sam here can radio ahead.'

Alex blew on his hands to get some circulation working; he was going to need good dexterity to manipulate the drill and insert the cannula directly into the bone marrow.

Meanwhile Beth wouldn't let go of Dennis's hand. She turned her head away as Alex got the drill out and winced at the sound.

But as they transferred him to the warmth and safety of the helicopter she blew out slowly. 'Do you think he's going to be okay?'

'If he is, it's thanks to you. But why did you come on your own when I told you to wait?'

She shook her head and her eyes blazed. 'Because I had to make sure the animals were okay.'

Now they were safe the reality of what had happened started to sink in and he fought the rising emotion born out of worry for her safety. 'You had a suspicion that he was feeding something nasty to his pets and you were going to confront him, right? Didn't you think for a moment that it might be dangerous?'

'I wanted to see for myself what was going on. I had to come, okay?'

'You should have waited.'

'What?' She blinked.

'You should have waited for me.' As he said it he saw the change in her demeanour; a shift to defensive and guarded. And he wished he could somehow take the words back. She was a professional and she'd been acting on a hunch. He had no doubt she would have dealt with the situation appropriately. It didn't mean he couldn't be worried about her, though.

'No, Alex. You don't get to tell me what to do. I didn't know how long you were going to be and I had to do something.' Her hands were shaking. They watched the helicopter rise and covered their faces from the dusting of snow. When the chopper had disappeared into cloud she sighed again. 'Turns out it was a lot more dangerous for him, not me.'

He touched her arm. 'I was worried about you.

I didn't know where you were or what had happened.'

'Now you know how it feels. And that was just for a few hours, not eight years.' She pressed her lips together and started to walk up the hill, her back taut and her feet stomping through the snow.

They'd both just been through something traumatic and intense and he knew she was spitting adrenaline-fuelled talk as a pressure release. But he also knew if they couldn't draw a line under what had happened then they'd never move forward. He'd thought they were moving forward. Technically, they were...but, just like on this ice, it was more like one step forward, three slips back. He caught up with her. 'Beth, please. For God's sake. I can't turn back the clock. I can't make what I did any different. I did it. I'm sorry. We don't have long before you head back to Glasgow. Can we please...*please* just have some time when you're not going to throw the past back at me?'

She stopped and turned to him. 'You hurt me.'

'I know. I know. And I'm trying to make things right.' He opened his arms wide, ignoring the whip of wind that brought the chill factor way below zero. And the fact she was wearing his coat, and his scarf had disappeared into the paramedics' detritus. So yes, he was standing on a hill, ankle-deep in snow, in a thin jumper and jeans, fast turning into a snowman, but he didn't care about any of that, because he cared too much for her and needed them to get past this. 'Want more target practice?'

She huffed out and pulled a face. 'It's no fun when the target is offering to *be* a target.'

'Okay, well, I'll walk ahead and you can take joy in the element of surprise. If that makes you feel better.'

'Stop being reasonable. It's annoying.' She fought a smile but not before he saw it. She'd always loved that he hit arguments head-on—that was probably another reason why she'd been so discombobulated when he'd backed right away all those years ago. What it meant, too, was that she still cared enough for him to be angry even now. He wasn't sure whether that was a warning or a gift but it certainly made his heart ache. Her shoulders sagged a little and he saw the chink in her armour that was shaped like him. 'I shouldn't have said what I said, Alex. I'm sorry. It was definitely mean after everything that's happened over the last few days. I think I'm a bit stressed out and emotional.'

'Understandable. Me too. But fighting each other isn't going to help.'

'I know. But the thing is, I don't know where

I am with you. I don't know how to feel. I like you. A lot. I'm just trying to work it all out.'

I like you. It was something. It was something he needed to think carefully about. He didn't want her getting ideas about things that simply couldn't happen, but he did want to smooth their relationship into something more than prickles. 'I'm at the point where feeling something is a distant memory. I'm numb. Completely numb.'

She scanned his face and upper body and winced. 'Oh, God, you're shivering.'

'Hypothermia tends to do that to a guy.'

Now she did smile. 'And you're joking about it. Here, have this.'

She went to slide her arms out of his coat but he stopped her. 'Keep it, there's no point in two of us freezing. But for the record, I don't know where I am with you either. I didn't intend for things to get complicated. I didn't intend to kiss you, but I'm bloody glad I did. And I want to do it again, if I can ever get my lips to defrost.'

'Here, you need to get warm.' She cupped both his hands in hers and blew on them until he wiggled them at her to show it was working.

'Beth, we need to talk about this. About what's happening.'

'Yes, we do. But not now. Not here. We need to get you somewhere warm.' She fastened her hand around one of his and started to trudge up the hill.

But he wasn't going to let this go. They needed to mark a line somehow on their past. 'Then when?'

'I don't know.' She opened and closed her mouth a couple of times as if trying to work out what to say and then, 'When you lifted that quad bike my heart was in my throat. You were bloody awesome.'

'Climbing gives you good upper-body strength.' He went to flex his muscles but couldn't make a fist; despite all her attempts at defrosting his hands were still pretty frozen.

'You've got good inner strength. That's what's even better. You make me smile, even when I'm trying to be cross at you. You didn't argue back, you just tried to take the sting out and it worked. And you gave me your coat.' She stopped walking, pulled his hands back to hers, looked deep into his eyes and smiled, pressing their hands to her heart. 'I know we need to talk about it and we will. But right now, before you freeze to death, I want you to know that even though I was very angry at you, I liked kissing you, too. A lot.'

He couldn't take his eyes off her. Standing here with water dripping from her hair, her cheeks burned with cold, her nose red, she was the most beautiful thing he'd ever seen and the frustration that she'd come up here to see Dennis on her own revealed itself to be because he cared for her. So much. Too much.

She smiled and then tiptoed so she was face to face with him. Mouth to mouth. Lips to lips. Her eyes misted and she brushed her cheek against his. 'In fact, I liked kissing you so much I'm going to do it again.'

'Good. It might help de-ice my mouth.'

'Oh, you know me, anything to help.' She slipped her arms around his neck and pressed against him. Then her mouth was on his, lips like ice but so damned sweet to taste.

He felt the outline of her body against his, the curve of her breast, the press of her hip, and the biting cold that had seeped deep into his bones was replaced with a heat so intense he struggled to control it. Fired by the mewl in her throat and the moan of pleasure on her lips he pushed her hair from her face, tilted her head and deepened the kiss, his tongue sliding against hers.

And she gripped his shoulders, fingernails deep as she raked down his back. As if the last eight years of wanting and aching and longing were wrapped up in this moment.

Whereas their last kiss had been a gentle exploration and reacquainting, this was electric and desperate. Greedy, open-mouthed, wet. And all he wanted was more of it. He ran his hands down her coat, inside her coat, pressing his palm over her breast.

'Alex.' She said his name like a plea and a promise and then she tugged away. Pressed her hands to his face and kissed his jaw, his cheek, his mouth, her breath coming in frenzied gasps. Then suddenly she was sliding and slipping away from him and he had to haul her up, clasping her against his side.

'This is treacherous.' She clung to his shoulders and he wondered whether he meant to her balance or to her heart. 'Damn ice.'

'I've got you.' And as he wrapped his arm round her waist to keep her upright he wished that were true. He wished he had her. He wished he could promise her all the things he knew she wanted.

But she laughed and shook him away. 'I'm fine. Honestly. I've got a grip now. I'm okay. We need to go.'

He tilted her chin so he could see her eyes. 'Are we good?'

'We're good. No more barbed comments.' She put her finger to her mouth and he noted her hand was shaking almost as much as he was. Then she tugged his coat round both their shoulders, wrapped her arm round his waist and started walking with him as if kissing as if your life depended on it and sliding ankle-deep in snow with an ex was perfectly routine in her life. She called out, 'Come on, Meg. Let's go get your girl.'

And he let it go. Because he had trouble keeping up with how they'd gone from her shooting metaphorical arrows at him to kissing, but trying to analyse something so impulsive and intense would break it.

Eventually, they made it down the track and back to the farm and she slid her hand out from his back, the cosy atmosphere broken by barking dogs and a sense of having to jerk right back into professional mode again. But he knew, and she knew, that out there on the hill they'd shared something precious.

She hurried towards the front door. 'Hey, I'll do you a coat swap if you can grab my jacket from the boot. I'll just get June and we can take her down to Angus along with Meg. Someone's going to have to look after them while Dennis is in hospital.'

'Sure thing.' It had been a hell of a day, and it was only three o'clock. His head was all over the place with the thought of Dennis's life-threatening injuries and then that scorching kiss. He couldn't keep the hell up. He took out his phone to call Maxine and explain why he was missing his clinic. He looked at the screen. No reception. Maybe it was worth a try anyway. Miracles did happen—Beth's kiss proved that.

As he tried to scroll through his contacts with fingers so cold they could barely move he opened Beth's car door with his other hand and something darted past him and out across the courtyard.

'What? Hey! Spike?' He stuffed his phone into his trouser pocket, bent to grab the pup but he'd already bounded well beyond his reach. 'Come here. Come back. Wait—'

As he ran to the door, Beth came running out of the house, saw Spike and screamed, tugging their puppy away from a bowl of food. 'No! Button, stop. Oh, Alex—'

The food. *Damn.* His gut contorted as a wave of nausea rippled through him. The only reason they'd come here was because they were concerned about the dog food and now Spike had eaten some.

'Oh, God, Beth. I didn't know he was in the car. I just opened the door and he jumped out.'

'I should have said. I was just distracted by everything.' She shook her head as tears glittered in her eyes. 'June's sick, Alex. I think maybe the food is contaminated. And now…did he…? Did Button eat any?'

Alex could barely swallow past the nausea but he wasn't going to sugar-coat the truth because she'd hate him if he did that. 'Some, I think. Before we managed to stop him.'

'He's a baby.' She pressed her lips together and for a moment he thought the entente between them was broken but she tugged on his hand, squeezing the way he imagined Dennis had squeezed before. As if her life depended on him. 'We need to get all three dogs to Angus.'

CHAPTER TEN

'I SHOULD BE in there.' Beth had spent every minute of the last two hours pacing the vet clinic
reception floor while Angus assessed Button in
the treatment room. Meg was fine and in a safe
pen. June was very sick and Beth had been allowed to take her bloods and X-rays but she'd
been ushered out when Angus had started the
charcoal stomach washout on Button.

'I'm the vet; you're the owner,' he'd said. 'Trust
me to do my job.' And she was trying to, but she
didn't know what to do with her hands and she
found herself literally wringing them together.
'What if he needs me?'

'You're going to wear a hole in the carpet.'
Alex stood up from the plastic chair and came
over to her. He put his hand on her shoulder and
she stopped moving, even though her thoughts
still whirred a mile a minute. 'Angus said it was
better that you weren't in there to see Button in

distress. He's got a good team with him. Come sit down.'

'But what if—'

'I'm not playing the what if game, Beth. Don't go there.' Having called his surgery and asked Fraser to cover the rest of his clinic, Alex hadn't left her side, as worried about the pup as she was.

For the millionth time today she fought the onslaught of tears. 'Hopefully, we got to him in time.'

'We did.' He looked into her eyes and smiled softly. 'Breathe, Beth. You're not going to be any use to him if you wear yourself out.'

He was right. She was going to need all her strength if their precious pup was sick...or worse. Following Alex's lead, she inhaled and breathed out slowly. Then she shook her hands out to try to relax them. 'It feels like a very long time since I set off this morning to take my mum to Bay View.'

He huffed out. 'Damn. I never even asked. How did it go?'

'She's happy as anything. She loves the room and the view and made fast friends with the lady in the room next to her. I ended up feeling like a spare part.' Which should probably have been a good thing, but Beth felt a little displaced. 'I mean, I'm glad she doesn't feel like a burden any more but is it bad to feel just a little bit...adrift?

Like my roots have been dug up and exposed. That everyone's got a life and I'm catching up.'

He walked her over to a chair, pushed her gently into it and sat next to her. 'I felt the same way when my folks upped and left. But you're strong, you'll deal with it.'

'After the day we've had I feel a lot more wobbly than strong, to be honest.'

'I'm never going to forget seeing the way you helped Dennis and willed him to hold on. Everything you did today was for someone else. You're amazing, Beth.' He tucked her hair behind her ear and whispered, 'But I already knew that. You've always been amazing.'

'So have you.' She'd watched in amazement as he'd lifted the quad bike from Dennis's leg. The calm, measured way he'd manipulated the drill and inserted a line that would surely have kept Dennis from slipping away. And she would never forget the look in his eyes of apprehension and relief when he'd run down the hill to her and the steadfast way he'd put his arms around her then. The way her heart had jittered and panicked and then calmed just at being in his arms.

Today had been a roller coaster of emotions but none so heightened as the desire she felt for this man right now. Things were getting back on track between them and they were developing a new way of being. And she liked it. She liked that they'd found each other again, but for eight years she'd wondered what had happened to him and why he'd so brutally cut her adrift. She'd discovered he'd been quietly facing the darkest part of his life, getting treatment and then growing into a good man, just as her mum had said. And she'd missed it.

That was what hurt the most. She'd missed those parts of his life and she would never get them back. She would never get the chance to show she could stick by him in times of duress. He'd taken that away from her.

So she could have railed against him the way she had on the hill, she could have made some snarky comment about the way he'd treated her. She could have said a million different things, but right now just being here with him was all that mattered. Holding each other up, taking comfort where it was offered.

He put his arm round her shoulders and she leaned against him, letting the tension ebb slightly. She snuggled closer into his arms, relishing the warmth of his body against hers, and wasn't surprised when she felt the press of his lips on her forehead. She turned her head and looked up at him. Saw the confusion in his eyes, but also the heat and the affection. They hadn't mentioned the kiss and she didn't know what to say about it now anyway. She'd gone with her gut, but ever since then her gut had been all messed up with her worrying about poor Button.

'Right, Beth, you have a choice.' It was Angus, bursting through the door in his usual brisk and efficient manner.

She jumped up, heart hammering against her rib cage as she looked at his empty hands. 'Is everything okay?'

'He's groggy and not at all pleased with me for the gastric lavage, but I think we've got everything out and his blood work was okay. I've repeated it and there's nothing to worry about... so far. But I don't have to tell you how quickly things can change, especially in babies. Right?'

She gripped Alex's hand. Tight. 'Right.'

'So...' Angus held the door open for them to walk through to the treatment area. 'I have my hands full with the overnighters we already have and now June too, and she's very sick so she's going to need a lot of my attention. Your choice—you can leave Button here with me to monitor him, or I'd be fine if you wanted to take him home to watch him yourself. Not something I usually allow, but because you're a vet it seems like a good plan.'

'Yes. Yes. Great plan. Let's take him.' Relief flowed thick through her veins and she couldn't move quickly enough. They found their boy fast asleep in one of the cages. She looked at his observation chart—everything was fine, as Angus said, *so far*. But if he'd absorbed any poison it could still be in his system. He wasn't out of danger yet.

Angus opened one of the cages and checked on June. Her observation chart told a very different story from Button's. 'I'm going to keep the other two here. June's still critical. Once she's better...' he gave a look that said *if* rather than *when* '... I'll foster them together until we know the outcome with Dennis.'

'Excellent.' Alex nodded and cautiously lifted a groggy Button out of the cage. 'Come on, then, boy. Time to go home.'

Angus laughed. 'Careful. He's tired and grumpy.'

'I know how he feels.' Alex smiled, relief in his features.

'And remember, even though his blood work's fine now, things could change. It's not as if we know what he might have ingested.'

'It doesn't bear thinking about.' Beth shuddered. Things could have been very different. 'Thanks for everything, Angus.'

'Not a problem. You've done enough for me these last few months.' The senior vet raised his stethoscope by way of a wave. 'Excuse me while I do another check on my charges.'

Beth walked with Alex and Button out into

Reception. 'Okay, as there's no room at this inn for the night I'll take him to mine.'

'Your furniture-less house?' Alex frowned. 'Absolutely not. If we're staying up all night we need some home comforts.'

'It's fine, I'll just keep him in my bedroom. Thankfully, my bed's still in there. That's about all, to be honest, but it means I have more space for him to run around.'

'No, Beth.' The pup was in the crook of one of his arms. Alex tilted her chin with his free hand, so she could see his eyes. That meant trouble. For her tummy if nothing else. Looking into his eyes made her hot and bothered and all kinds of jittery. 'We can't all squeeze into your child-hood bed.'

'We?' The thought of them all in her bedroom gave her hives. Not that spending the night with Alex hadn't crossed her mind…it had. Many times. But not under these circumstances. 'It'll be just me and Button.'

Alex shook his head vehemently. 'No, no. I have custody of him at night, that's the arrange-ment. He's used to falling asleep on my chest— er…bed. Besides, my house is closer to the clinic in case we need to dash back over with him. He has to come to mine.'

Infuriating man. She shook her chin free from his fingers. 'But I'm the vet, Alex. He's been released into my care, not yours. I need to monitor him.'

He was cradling the dog against his chest as if it was the most precious gift he'd ever been given. 'Then maybe you can come too. What do you think, Spike?'

The pup sleepily nuzzled against her hand. She decided it was an overwhelming yes. 'Well, thank you.' She laughed. 'That will work.'

'Just don't distract us. We have a routine.'

'Okay, I'll try to keep low-key.' She rolled her eyes. Infuriating, sexy man. Funny too.

They walked out into the dark evening. Alex bundled the puppy into his car then turned to her, placing his hands on her shoulders, relief morphing into serious. 'Listen, I'm sorry, Beth.'

'For being a royal pain in the backside?'

'For letting him out of the car.' He looked, as he'd looked on and off since they'd found Button nose down in the food bowl, bereft. Without second-guessing herself she reached up to him and put her hand to his cheek. 'It's not your fault. None of it.'

He shook his head. 'I should have thought he'd be in the car.'

'I should have said. We were both distracted by Dennis's accident. Let's not play the blame game, eh?' She needed him right now—he was the only person in the world who cared for Button as much as she did, no matter how much they'd both decided not to get attached. Alex was the only person she could share this worry with.

'Thank you.' He cupped her face and dropped a kiss on the tip of her nose. 'We should get that boy home.'

'Wait.' She looked at his kind eyes and that sexy mouth that she knew so intimately and the swell of emotion in her chest was almost too much to bear. The bond wasn't just with Button, it was with Alex. A bond that had been broken but not irrevocably. There was hope. There was desire.

Then, she was kissing him, pressing her body against the length of his. Being in his arms was safe and comfortable and yet felt as if she were stepping into somewhere exotic at the same time. Familiar but exciting. She felt his arms snake around her waist and he pushed her back against the car. And thank God he did, because her legs were like jelly and her head dizzy with the sensation of his mouth on hers. It felt as if she'd been eight years in the wilderness and she'd finally come home. This was her homecoming gift: this kiss. This man. It didn't matter what difficulties they'd overcome or those they were going to face, this moment mattered more.

When he pulled back he was breathless. He ran the backs of his fingers down her cheek.

'Hey, you're shivering—you still haven't thawed out properly?'

'Just call me Ice. Ice baby.' She was only half joking, because her clothes were still damp from kneeling in the snow, although not as damp as his. She put her hand under his jumper and pressed it against the heat of his belly.

'What the hell, Freckles?' He squirmed away from her. 'What is it with you and the hot and cold treatment?'

And she couldn't help smiling because he hadn't called her Freckles for such a long time and it was right and perfect and she didn't want to stop the way she was feeling: comfortable with him, proud of what they'd done to save Dennis, worried about Button and not just a little turned on to have touched Alex's bare torso.

It took five minutes to reach Alex's house, five minutes of fighting the urge to make him stop the car and kiss him again, but they had precious cargo and they needed to get him home and safe.

Memories flooded in as she carried Button into the cottage. How many hours, days, weeks had she spent in here over her lifetime? How many dinners had she shared with his family, laughing with his sister, talking about her studies with his parents? She could draw the timber framing with her eyes closed, describe the layout of the kitchen.

And yet it was the same but different. 'You've painted it. It looks great. Fresh.'

'Thanks.' He smiled and something kicked in her chest. 'It needed a lot of work. My dad was a great doctor but he's not the DIY type.'

She hadn't thought Alex would have been either, and yet there was a new window seat exactly where she would have put one, although it woefully lacked cushions. And the wall colours were muted greys where she would have chosen something a little bolder. It was a man's house. Smart and clean and…it smelt of him. Her tummy clenched. Spending the night here was going to be hell. And would test every part of her resolve.

Although, given the fact she'd already kissed him twice today she had a feeling she'd badly failed the resolve test already.

'Put him down here. I'll light the fire.' Alex stroked Button's head and pointed to a rug on the hearth. Just seeing that rug brought memories tumbling back.

'Is that your nana's old rug?'

The one they'd made out on many times when his family had been away, in front of a roaring fire; heat and heat and heat. There had never been anything wrong with the passion and attraction. Just the trust, it would appear. But she could feel that changing.

He bundled kindling and newspaper into the fireplace and threw a lit match onto it. The kindling sparked and little blue-orange flames erupted. He dragged a fireguard out and put it in front of the fire to protect Button from errant sparks. 'It's part of her rug, yes. The part Spike has allowed me to keep. I'm going to have to ask Joe's new wife Rose if she can do her crochet magic and fix it so it doesn't look so ragged.' Rose was infamous in Oakdale for her bright-coloured yarn bombs around the village. Beth decided that if she lived in this house she'd definitely be asking Rose for something to brighten it up. A stripy blanket and multicoloured cushions. And there she was, making plans she was never going to keep. Alex smiled. 'Or maybe I'll have to bin it like the rest of the stuff we used to have in here.'

'It's very minimal. Have you been watching that tidying programme on TV too?'

He laughed. 'I don't need to. When my parents moved overseas we had a big sort out. Although, I have to admit to being ruthless. What they needed for a flat in Malaga and what they wanted me to have didn't compute. It was like they wanted to keep all their old stuff here as a sort of shrine to them. I wasn't having any of that.'

'Sounds just like my mum.' She sat down on a

smart charcoal-grey sofa that had some very un-puppy-friendly pristine white blankets folded up on the arm. The puppy tsunami must have been a big wake-up call for him. 'I like what you've done to the place. You were working in London, though. Why did you come back to live here?'

He rocked back on his heels and absent-mindedly stroked Button's back as he talked. 'It was my dad who suggested it. He was think-ing about retiring and wanted someone to take over and asked if I'd ever considered coming home. Home. It hadn't felt like home for a long time. I'd keep coming back and you weren't here. Anywhere that didn't feature you wasn't my home.' He swallowed and smiled ruefully. 'I went through all that and couldn't have you anyway.'

'Oh, Alex.' This was getting to the nub of things. Honesty. Finally. Her throat felt raw.

He shuffled over to sit on the floor by the sofa, tugged off one of her boots and socks and started to massage her toes. 'I was adrift for a bit after the treatment. I was working in the East End and I just couldn't settle but felt like I'd been given a second chance and that I had to choose wisely. I needed to leave all those bad memories behind. I wanted to…indulge myself, I guess. I love the hills and the mountains and the fishing and boating. I figured if I hated working here I could move on again. Two years later, I'm still here.'

She was stuck on imagining him in treatment. She shuddered, suddenly very cold. 'Was it bad? As bad as Mikey?'

His hand stilled. 'Yes. And no. I knew what was to come. I'd walked it all with my cousin.'

A gruelling treatment regime. Surgery. Chemo. Radiotherapy. But Mikey had had Alex by his side all the way and Alex had done it on his own.

She wanted to reach out and hold him close but she got the feeling he didn't want her comfort for what had happened. He'd made his choice and he'd had to live with it. The only physical contact was his hand on her foot. Massaging her toes was something he used to do for her years ago after they'd been hiking and her boots had rubbed. Her mind seemed to be endlessly spinning from the past to the present. So much of her formative years had been spent with him she couldn't disentangle herself. As he'd been able to do with her. 'I'm sorry I wasn't there, Alex.'

He snagged her gaze. His was filled with regret and longing and a plea to forget it all. 'Beth, please—'

She reached for him now, clutching him tight against her. 'No, this isn't me being angry. This is me being genuinely sorry I wasn't there. For you. I wish we could rewind and change what happened.'

'Trust me, I wish that too. But you're here now. That's enough for me.'

A beeping made them both jump and, cursing, he pulled his phone from his pocket. 'The hospital. I'll just take this.' He looked at Button, who had stirred at the noise. 'In the kitchen, so I don't disturb him.'

He came back a few minutes later with two glasses of wine that he set on the coffee table, before sitting on the sofa next to her. He looked ashen and shaken and she wasn't sure whether it was because of the phone call or the memories of his dark days.

'Dennis?' Her heart thrummed and her gut tightened in readiness for bad news.

But Alex gave her a small smile. 'Yes. They called me because I was put down as a contact. They have no next of kin for him.'

'He really is all alone. Poor guy. But still alive?' The knots in her stomach eased a little. But she still had to reconcile the reason she'd been at the farm in the first place with the sick man in the hospital bed.

'He's in Intensive Care. They've had to amputate his leg. It's very early days and he's critical but they think he'll recover.'

'I don't suppose he said anything about his dogs and what was making them ill?'

'Nothing. They've put him in an induced coma. He won't be talking for a while.'

'Maybe we'll never know. I did some Internet searching yesterday and I read about Munchausen by proxy in pet owners and it *is* a thing. There have been some cases where people have made their animals sick to get attention.' Just the thought of it made her shudder. 'I don't want to say that was what he was doing, but hopefully we'll get the test results back from the food sample I sent off and we'll find out. We did good.'

He picked up his glass and drank. 'We make a good team. Medically, I mean. In small country places like this it's good for different health professionals to share information. You probably saved his life. Your trick of getting Meg onto his chest would have kept him warm.'

'He needed something to hang on for and I know that—whatever he's done or not done to them—he does love his animals.' She wondered what Alex had had to hold on for. Because it certainly hadn't been for her. He'd decided to face it on his own. Geez, she couldn't imagine what torture that would have been. And instead of being angry with him she just felt a huge sense of sadness. And relief that he was here and well.

'And good news that Spike—' He put his glass

on the table. 'He needs a proper name, Beth. We can't keep calling him Button and Spike. It's confusing. It's confusing me. We need a name everyone can call him, even when he goes to his new place. He needs his own name. Just one, right?'

Everything was confusing. That she was here in this house, that her foot was snuggled in Alex's hands. That she couldn't think of anyone else she'd rather spend the night with watching over a sick puppy. Anyone she'd rather spend the night with. Period. And now they were choosing a for-ever name for a pet they weren't going to keep. She'd already thought about this. 'Could we just call him Boy?'

'Is Boy a real name?'

As he said it the pup's ears twitched and he raised his head and looked at them. Alex laughed. 'That's decided, then. Boy it is. I like it.'

He took her other foot and pulled the boot off and his hands began their massage magic. For a moment she was lost in the rhythm of his touch. He removed her sock and began massaging her instep, each stroke sending shivers of desire up her legs and arrowing deep in her belly. She lay back and let his fingers explore her toes, her calf and she imagined his fingers higher and the pleasure he could give her. Not just with his fingers…

And then…and then what?

'What are we doing?' She pulled her legs up and hugged her knees.

He growled, his hands splayed as if asking *what the actual hell?* 'It's just feet, Beth.'

It wasn't just feet. They both knew damned well it wasn't about the feet. It was about the contact, about the touching and where it would lead. Not that she didn't want to go to bed with him, but what then? Would they do the long-distance thing as they'd done at uni? Would they—? Her ricocheting thoughts stalled as his hand ran up her leg, stopping just above her knee. 'Your jeans are still damp. You have to take them off before you catch cold. I have something you can wear instead. Wait here.'

He was back in minutes, having changed into some track pants and a clean dry T-shirt, and carrying a pile of freshly laundered clothes. She eyed him suspiciously and laughed. 'This is the scene in the rom-com movie where you hand me your clothes, I smell your amazing smell and then fall into bed with you, right?'

Okay, perhaps suspiciously *and* a little hopefully.

His eyebrows rose. 'If that's what you want. Sure. But, hand on heart, it wasn't what I was thinking.'

'Oh, no? What were you thinking?'

He handed her the clothes and sat down next to

her. Closer than before. 'I was wondering if I had enough washing powder for our clothes and then I was calculating if I put the washing machine on now what time the cycle would be finished.'

'Really? So the foot massage wasn't…?' She'd been daydreaming about sex when he'd honestly been all about the massage?

'Beth.' He flashed a smile, his hand back on her leg. 'I was hoping you'd go for a shower to warm up, maybe invite me to join you. Then I'd hand you my shirt and you'd slide it on and look even more sexy than you actually do. If that was physically possible.'

Her mouth went all kinds of dry…and wet. 'Um, really?'

'And then, later, after we'd eaten oysters and drunk champagne, I'd get to peel it off you and you'd be so overwhelmed by my scent—not my smell. If you were overwhelmed by my smell then I'd have to use more deodorant—'

She giggled. 'You don't need more deodorant. You smell like Alex. I don't want you to smell like anything else.'

'And then we'd fall into bed.'

'You do want to go to bed with me.' It wasn't a question. She just had to say it out loud.

'Yes.' He put his hand to the back of her head and drew her to him, lowering his mouth to her neck. 'I have never stopped wanting to go to bed with you, Beth Masters. Not once in eight years. Going to bed with you is at the top of my bucket list. Only, I don't have oysters. Or champagne. Just this wine.'

'Wine works.' She'd be gone soon enough, then this would be over. Could they? Should they? Could they put the past behind them? She pressed against him, her hands on the cool cotton covering his taut plane of a stomach, wishing she were running her hands over bare skin. She swallowed hard. 'We can't.'

His mouth moved to her throat and kissed a trail to her collarbone that made her dizzy and heady and frantic for more. 'You're going to Glasgow and it's complicated and your life is there and mine is here and we should be old enough to control our sex drives, right?'

'I mean...' She could barely breathe for the rush of sensation over her skin, in her body, making her breath ragged. Needy, desperate. 'We can't go upstairs and leave Boy here. In case he's poorly.'

'He's sleeping now. We can leave him for a few minutes.'

'Is that all it's going to take?' She pushed his shoulder, wanting that mouth on hers. Hot damn, how much longer was she going to have to wait? 'Eight years and I get a few minutes?'

She couldn't keep up with the rapid-fire beat

of her heart and the deluge of emotions rushing through her. It felt as if all the arguing, the missing him, the raging on the hill had led to this moment. She knew how he kissed; she knew how he made love. Rather, she remembered how he was then. How would he make love now? Would he be more confident? More skilled?

She wanted to know. Now. She sat up, put her hands on his shoulders and straddled him. She wanted to relearn him. This could be her last chance. Her only chance to be with him. She could do it. Let the embers flare and then douse them when she left to go back to Glasgow. If she didn't, she'd always regret missing this chance. She was going to do this. She was going to take what she wanted and she was going to walk away with her heart intact. Her eyebrows rose and she nodded towards the sleeping puppy.

'Boy,' she whispered, testing the viability of the plan.

The dog didn't flinch, twitch or move so much as a muscle.

She turned to Alex, drank him in, a sigh escaping her throat. 'He's fast asleep.'

'Good, because he's far too young to witness this.' Then he pulled her down to him and crushed her mouth in a scorching kiss.

This was no relearning; it was taking and giving. It was greedy. Demanding. It was a lifeline of hope, a prayer. And she melted into it. Into him. She felt his hands wrap round her, settling her higher onto his lap. She felt his hardness underneath her and rocked against it, wanting him inside her with a savage need she'd never felt before. His hands skimmed under her still-damp jumper and ripped it from her, then he was palming her breasts through her bra. 'You have no idea how much I have wanted this. How long I have waited for this. For you.'

She pressed herself against his erection, tugging at the waistband of his track pants, but he covered her hand with his. 'Wait.'

She pulled back, her mouth throbbing from the delicious roughness of his kisses. Was he having second thoughts? 'What's wrong?'

His eyes darted to Boy and he shook his head. 'I'm getting stage fright. Come on.'

And with that he slid his arms under her legs and lifted her, powering up the stairs two at a time. He kicked open the master bedroom door and she was momentarily afraid it would be the same as she remembered: all nineteen-eighties flowered curtains and chenille bedspread. But it was decorated in the same chic masculine tones as downstairs with a very modern bed and she breathed. 'I thought we were going to be having sex in chintz.'

'Kinky too?' His eyes glittered. 'Sorry to disappoint.'

'No way, Alex. I'm far from disappointed.'

'And I haven't even started yet.' He laid her on the thick cream faux-wool blanket and she felt as if she were sinking into heaven. More so when he unzipped her jeans and slowly peeled them from her. Her breath hitched as he climbed onto the bed, crawling over her body until his mouth was on hers again, stealing more hot kisses as he unclipped her bra.

Her thoughts blurred as he slid cool fingers over her nipples, his playful demeanour slipping into something serious. He looked at her as if she were a goddess, as if the pleasure was all his and he couldn't quite believe his luck. 'You've grown into one hell of a woman, Beth.'

He lowered his mouth and licked her nipple, making her moan in desperation and delight. He teased her by pulling his mouth away, making her cry out in desperation for more. Then he lavished both breasts with kisses until her thoughts fled and she could only feel. His touch. His mouth. The way every part of her body strained for him.

Rising up on her knees, she slid his trousers and then boxers over strong muscular thighs, releasing his erection. He groaned as she took him in her hand and looked down at the man he'd become. Half cautious, half curious.

'I…?' She didn't know what she'd thought. Maybe that he'd look different. But he was all there.

He took her hand and brought her to face him. 'Amazing what they can do.'

'Amazing indeed.' She went to reach for him again, but he flipped her on her back and kissed a trail of wet kisses down her abdomen. She writhed against him, anticipation of his tongue at her core making her crazy with need. He parted her legs and slipped his fingers deep and she clenched around them, fighting the rising release. But when she felt the scorching heat of his mouth against her nub and his fingers sliding she knew the fight was lost. Losing hold of her control, she sobbed out, 'Alex. I need… I need you.'

Not just this, but everything. She needed his strength. She needed his kisses. She needed him. Now and always.

'I need you too. You have no idea.' He gripped her tight as she shuddered against him, his hair in her fingers, his name on her lips. *Alex. Alex. Alex.* So many times she'd dreamt about this, believing it could never happen again. And here he was. Wrapped around her, clutching her tight against him as if she were his everything.

But it wasn't enough. She wanted him inside her, on her. With her. She tugged him up to her and kissed him hard, stroking his length. He groaned into her mouth. 'Wait. Slow down.'

No. 'I'm done waiting. I've waited too long.'

'Condom.' His hand flailed out to the drawer in the cabinet by the bed and he grabbed a foil.

'I thought...?' She watched him slide it on, confused. Desperate. Not wanting to think about anything except the next minute. She didn't know what she thought. Good. Condom. Good.

He laid her back on the fur and positioned himself at her entrance. His eyes blazed his truth, the same truth in her heart. The same truth she'd carried for over a decade. 'Are you sure?'

'More than anything.' She shifted beneath him, shocked and exhilarated at the feel of him against her. She wrapped her legs around him as he slid deep into her. At the first thrust he inhaled sharply, closed his eyes as if in prayer, whispering, 'Beth. My Beth.'

He smoothed her hair back and kissed her with such urgency she thought her heart might stop. He thrust again. And again, holding her hands above her head. 'I want to see you. I have missed you so much. My Beth. My beautiful Beth.'

She'd planned to do this and keep her heart intact. She wasn't going to let him have any of it. But it was too late. She bit back a sob, but couldn't stop the tears pricking her eyes. He was the beautiful one. He was divine; he was hers.

It was the same. It was different. It was a new stamp on her heart. A soft bruise on her soul. An ache that would never be fully satisfied.

She arched and encouraged him deeper, learning what he liked now. Learning what made him groan with pleasure. And in return he teased and tormented, his rhythm tantalisingly slow then deep, then fast, and with each new stroke her heart accepted him more, her body shaped herself to him.

He wiped the tears from her cheek, pressed his mouth to each one, a sound in his throat equal to hers. A sob. A cry. Then his rhythm increased and he thrust fast and deep. Wild. Untamed. The grief and the need and the ache of eight long years written on his face, in his pace. She sat up and pulled him to sit facing her, wrapped her legs around his hips, gripping his shoulders so he could go deeper still. The intensity was like nothing else she'd ever experienced. His eyes locked onto hers, his fist wound into her hair. She let the tears flow freely, couldn't stop them when he called her name into the dark and shuddered against her, his loss of control stoking hers. They grasped, kissed, clung to each other as release bonded them closer. Tighter.

For ever.

CHAPTER ELEVEN

'THAT WAS AMAZING.'

Beth peeled herself away and lay, breathless, on his bed. Alex felt the damp of her tears as they dried on his clavicle. 'Amazing' didn't get near to describing how it felt. She'd brought light into his life, she'd pushed against his barriers, she'd made him feel, made him want. Made his heart ache.

He'd broken his promise—not to have sex with anyone who cared more than he did. Beth cared. He could see it in the way she looked at him: as if he was something good. As if he was beautiful too.

He couldn't remember anyone ever looking at him like that, as if he were an actual freaking superhero. It made the centre of his chest raw and tight as if there were light in there, and warmth. As if he could do anything. It wasn't the kind of feeling he'd had when the surgeon had said he'd successfully removed the lump, or when the oncologist had said he was cancer-free. This was a whole different kind of feeling, that someone believed he was good, that she believed in him. That everything he'd done and been through had been for this moment, for her.

And hell, he cared. Cared more than he wanted to admit. Cared more than ever before. And he wanted to keep on having that feeling.

And yet…it was impossible. For him to be happy meant she couldn't be.

She stroked his chest with trembling fingers, which he captured with his. Tears still lingered in her eyes and she looked a mixture of happy and kind of weirded out. He kissed her forehead. 'Are you okay?'

She smiled. 'I think so. It's just been so… much. I'm having trouble dealing with it all. You?'

I don't know.

'Yes. Yes, of course. Intense. Exhausted, actually.' He cuddled closer and tried to push the nagging thoughts away.

She pressed against him and laughed softly, her palm on his chest, over his heart. 'Oh? You're a…what did Frank call it? A tupped-out ram. Do I need to be careful?'

'Trust me, your liver and spleen are safe. But I can't vouch for anything else.' He ran fingertips over her nipples, loving the way they budded at his touch. He ran his hands down her curves, and he looked at her skin in the shaft of moonlight fingering through the open blinds. If this was going to end—and they both knew it would— he was going to make it the gentlest ending ever. Not like last time. 'How many more freckles are there now?'

She giggled against his ribs. 'Infinity has no end.'

Like the feeling in his chest that was so intense he wasn't sure he would breathe properly again. He stroked down her side, stopping at a whorl of purple on her hip bone. 'What are these? Bruises?'

She shrugged. 'Must be from falling in the snow when I was at Dennis's farm. I was more on the ground than upright. I should have just gone roly-poly down that hill.'

'God, you put your all into everything you do. You always did.' She was so beautiful and he had to tell her, show her what he felt, just once. 'I didn't think we'd ever…get this chance again. I just wish we'd had more time.'

She tilted her head to look at him, her hair tickling his neck. Her eyes tear-stained but dry now and ardent. 'We have time, Alex. We have a few more days before I go back. Then…who knows what could happen? It's not far to Glasgow.'

He did not want to say this, but he had to. He'd told her enough for her to not get any ideas that this could be anything more than temporary. Even though temporary wasn't what he wanted. 'We both know this can't go anywhere.'

'It feels like you've already decided.' She kept on looking at him as if she could see the very depths of his soul. 'Tell me.'

This was the *talking about it* that they'd agreed on yesterday. She wanted to know about the treatment, about everything. She wanted to know about everything he wanted to forget. She wanted to know where they stood now and what the future held.

And ruin this moment? *No, thank you.* He pushed the sheets back and stood up, pulling on some boxers, suddenly too aware of the gaping chasm between what they wanted and what they could actually have. 'We need to go downstairs to check on Boy.'

But she kept on looking at him and they both knew he was stepping back from his usual forthright Alex and hedging.

'Okay. Yes. Come on, then.' She wrapped a blanket round her shoulders and wandered back downstairs clutching two pillows. He followed, carrying two more. She was naked, but for the blanket wrap, her hair hung down her back in loose honey curls and her mouth was bruised and swollen from kissing. She knelt to stroke Boy, who was clutching his saggy green and yellow toy duck in his front paws. Alex wondered if it was possible to die from feeling too much. Because if it was, he was probably in his last minutes on Earth right now.

'Is he okay?'

'Sound asleep.' She plumped up the pillows and put them at one end of the sofa, then threw the blankets down, devising a makeshift bed. She climbed in and beckoned for him to follow.

He climbed in next to her, slid his arm under her and tugged her to his chest. He could hardly believe it. She was here in his arms. Christmas come early. Christmas. His heart clenched.

Not now. Don't spoil it. Be gentle.

'This is even smaller than your bed.'

She wiggled her hip against him. 'Cosy. I like it.'

And he had to admit, the glowing space in his chest was filled with warmth and a feeling he didn't want to end. She breathed against him, hooking her arm over his abdomen. 'Given Mikey's history, didn't you do regular checks for lumps?'

So if he thought he was off the hook he was sorely mistaken. He knew her well enough that she wasn't going to give up. He stared into the darkness. Thinking about the past and the future that had been stolen from him. Her future too. He owed her this talk.

'I did checks, of course. Regular and thorough. Then I got busy with the clinical rotations at the hospital. Working long hours with no sleep for days was hard and there was the studying on top. Routines become non-existent and it's just a case of trying to survive. You lose track of the days and…you get blasé. You see people who are sick and you know you're not like them. You begin to think you're bulletproof.'

'You should be able to think like that when you're young.'

'And then one day it occurred to me that I hadn't even thought about it. That should have been a good thing, right? That I was getting through the grief of losing Mikey. And so I did the usual checking…' The day he'd found the lump had been one of his darkest. He hadn't needed a specialist to tell him what it was. 'I just hadn't realised it could spread so quickly. It was aggressive.'

She squeezed against him and took his hand, lacing her fingers into his. 'Didn't they offer sperm banking?'

The real nub of it all now. Could she have the future she wanted and with him? Was this even a scenario she could imagine?

Had they mentioned saving his sperm? 'Everything from that day is a blur—except the diagnosis. It was as if the consultant had just said cancer, cancer, cancer, cancer and nothing else. I remember the panic that filled my whole body. The cold of the ultrasound jelly. The feel of the oxygen mask on my face. The taste of the anaesthetic as I drifted to sleep. I think they did talk about sperm banking…but I don't remember saying yes. I was too worked up to get the damned tumour out of me. I wasn't thinking straight. I was blinded by panic. I thought I was going to die, Beth. I thought I was going to face months of treatment and then things would get worse and then that would be the end. You have no idea the kind of things you feel—or don't feel—when you're staring at the prospect of dying. Of how much living you still want to do and you don't have time.'

He remembered the phone call he'd made, willing himself to stay calm and sound normal. Blunt but normal. Trying to stop Beth from crying when his own tears were streaming down his cheeks. The thought he might never see her again and that he was glad that he'd saved her from all this mess.

Then, the wait for his parents and feeling so alone.

'I would have been panicked too.' She kissed his knuckles. 'And now? Now the panic is over?'

'I haven't been tested in a few years, but the last test said I had zero chance of getting a woman pregnant. And the test before that. Every test, Beth. Post-treatment fertility levels vary and sometimes they recover. So far mine hasn't. There are no guarantees. I can't say what will happen.' He needed to get this through to her. This was why he'd refused to make meaningful connections with any woman. 'I don't want to make promises I can't keep.'

She stared into the dying embers in the grate. 'It doesn't all have to be your decision, Alex.'

'I'm not going to let anyone martyr themselves over me. Okay? I don't want pity.' He wanted her love. He wanted to be the man she wanted, deserved. And he just couldn't be.

'Give me a chance to prove that there is nothing like pity in here.' She put her hand on her chest. 'But there's a whole lot of something and I know you feel it too. Something good, something that's not going to go away any time soon.'

She pressed her lips together and he wondered if she was holding back more tears. When she turned to him he saw that she was and his heart melted all over again. He smoothed her hair back and kissed her cheek. 'Let's not talk about the future. Let's just do the present.'

She put her hand to his chest. 'I like the present.'

'Me too. I like you, Beth Masters. So damned much.' He didn't want to talk any more. Or think.

He just wanted to lose himself in her. Cupping her face, he slid his mouth over hers. This kiss was filled with everything he wanted to tell her. His regret, his feelings for her, which were currently a lot more than like on the affection scale. He wanted to make the most of what they had left even though he knew spending more time with her would make it so much harder to walk away in the end. But, for now, he was going to live in the present and think about the future another day.

Just as things were getting interesting she jerked and kicked out her leg. 'Ugh! What the hell is that? Button—I mean, Boy? What the heck? He's nudging his nose on my hip.'

Alex laughed. 'He does that when he needs a wee.'

'I'll take him.' Sighing, she went to stand but he slid from the sofa and wrapped a lap blanket round his waist. 'No, I will. I'll let him out in the garden. Stay right there. Do not go to sleep. Do not pass go...we have more catching up to do.'

'I am far from sleep, Dr Norton.' She shivered and pulled the covers up to her shoulders. 'But what about our little puppy audience?'

He grinned, his heart full, a little panicked by the weight in his chest and a lot turned on. 'Didn't you know? That's why blankets were invented.'

* * *

'Alex—?' Beth felt about for his warm body and found nothing but space next to her on the sofa. He'd gone. Her heart trembled. Gone where? Was that it? Over so soon? She sat up and blinked, and the panic subsided. 'Oh.'

He was curled up asleep, at the far end of the sofa, his bare chest covered by a snoozing puppy. Soft dawn light filtered through the blinds, bathing them in a halo of gold. Oh, God, could he be any sexier? Her chest flooded with warmth just to look at them, so completely relaxed.

This was how things could have been—him, a pet or two and further down the line some kids. The family she'd always craved. Her heart felt as if it were turning in on itself. That wasn't going to happen, not with Alex. If he asked, would she put that dream aside?

She didn't know. She couldn't say. How did you stifle your ticking body clock?

They'd missed eight years, and yet would she have felt like this if she'd walked his cancer journey beside him? Would she honestly have stayed the duration? She liked to think she would have, but she didn't know. She'd have given up her course to look after him, the way he'd taken a six-month break to look after Mikey, but then what?

In the meantime, she'd finished her degree and

got a whole load of experience. She'd grown independent, without him. She'd grown out of the break-up and now she knew what she wanted and what she was prepared to take and also what she wasn't prepared to give up. Could she give up her dream? For the man who'd already broken her heart?

Would he ask?

Alex stirred and uncurled, one hand clasping Boy to his stomach. 'Beth. You're still here. Good. Very good. Sleep okay?'

'The best for a long time.' She stretched over and kissed them both, pausing to nuzzle into Boy's soft silk coat. 'You?'

'We had three wees overnight and a little play at four-thirty...until five fifty-two.' He didn't look cross, just mussed-up and sleepy and very much in love with his dog. 'There is absolutely nothing wrong with this animal.'

'Good. That's so good to hear.' Her heart was filled with relief. And yet a sadness she couldn't shake. 'But playing at night-time? Really? Why didn't you wake me?'

He stroked her leg and his eyes crinkled with fun. 'I need you to have all the energy you can muster.'

'Oh? What for?'

'You know what for.' He tiptoed his fingers up her thigh, making her gasp. She crawled into his arms, her breasts puckering against his bare skin. It was impossible to refuse him.

Because she definitely knew what for. He'd shown her what for, under the blankets. Twice. And she'd relished every stroke and every kiss. She loved the way he made her feel. She loved the way he looked at her.

So why break it all with questions? They had no idea what was going to happen. Who did? You could make plans and be knocked over by a truck tomorrow. She was going to enjoy this ride, for as long as it lasted. Which, she considered with an ache in her chest, was going to be until Christmas Day when she pointed her car towards Glasgow.

She snuggled against him, breathing in the man and fussing over the dog. It was perfect. For now. She struggled with the catch in her throat. Damned emotions, she still hadn't worked out how to declutter them.

Alex looked quite pleased with himself as he said, 'I need you to be bright-eyed and bushy-tailed for a date.'

'Oh? Really?' That was a surprise.

He nodded. 'Boy wants to go to the Christmas markets in Carlisle, so I promised we'd take him.'

She couldn't hide her smile. 'So, it's a date for Boy really, not for me.'

'He said you could come. If you behaved yourself.'

She laughed, because how could she not? 'But you don't like Christmas. The same way I don't like Christmas. It has too many memories.'

His eyes clouded and he stroked her cheek. 'Oh, Beth. I am so sorry. I know that's my fault.'

She shrugged, telling herself it didn't matter any more. Trying to believe it. 'It's okay. Honestly. Each Christmas is different and it's up to us to make them good ones.'

'Exactly. And Boy doesn't have any experience of the festive thing, so we're going to educate him.' He leaned in and kissed her. 'And I want to make things better.'

She took a deep breath. 'They are better.'

'Good.' He jumped up and put the puppy on the floor, then tugged her to standing. He wrapped his arms around her and kissed her deeply until she was moaning his name and wanting more. But he pulled away and smiled. 'Right, you go shower. I'll make breakfast.'

'You cook too? That's new. I like the new you, Alex Norton.'

'It's muesli, don't get too excited.' He squeezed her bottom. 'And I like you more, Elizabeth Grace.'

She tucked that away and almost danced up the stairs. It was stupid to let her heart jump at his words. He'd broken her and he could do it again.

But forewarned was forearmed and she was stronger now. She knew not to invest too much and she was trying hard not to. She turned the shower tap on high and stood under the hosing water until her skin was red and the soft aches from their lovemaking were eased a little and she'd gathered herself together and got her head in the right space for a day at work.

When she sauntered back into the bedroom he was waiting for her. Her skin prickled at the sight of him, in anticipation of a smile, a kiss, sex. 'Oh? Wanting to join me? Sorry, I just got out. I can go back in…?'

'No. Beth.' He was holding the phone in his hand, his face pale. Something was wrong. Something bad. Her heart thumped and she clutched the towel tight around her, all thoughts of sex and kisses chased away. Ice slid into her chest. 'Was that the hospital again? Is it about Dennis?'

He swallowed. Shook his head. His eyes were sad. So sad. 'No.'

'Then what? What's the matter? Are you sick? Is it my mum?'

'No.' He took her to the bed and sat her down, stroking her cheek. 'It was someone asking to adopt Boy.'

'No.' Her heart slammed against her rib cage. 'They can't.'

'They can. We advertised. We asked everyone to put the word out.' He blinked, his lashes damp, his breathing uneven. He cleared his throat. 'A family. Two small children who desperately want a puppy for Christmas.'

'It's for life, Alex. Not just the festive season.'

He held her and rocked her close. 'They sound nice, Beth. They have a farm, so he has lots of space to play and run around.'

She clenched her fists, trying not to cling to him. She didn't want to be needy. She didn't want to feel so much about either of them. But it was too late. She'd fallen in love with Boy and…no. She wasn't going to admit that the way she felt about Alex was anything more than a crush. An infatuation. A sexy walk down Memory Lane. She wasn't in love with him. But her heart was still breaking. 'When? When do they want him?'

'They're coming to collect him tonight. After work. It's Christmas in three days and they want to have him as soon as possible.'

She fought back tears. 'So soon?'

'It's for the best, eh?' Alex's voice broke slightly and she realised he was hurting as much as she was. And yet was trying to be gentle with her. 'Better to let him go now before we get too attached.'

Which was what she'd thought about doing with Alex, but when it came to it, she knew it would be so hard to let him go too. 'But I'm on call tonight. I can't be here to meet them—' Or make sure they were the right fit for her puppy.

She swallowed through a raw throat, unable to find any more words. It was what they'd decided, back at the beginning. Neither of them could take on a puppy long term and when she was back in Glasgow he'd have no one to take over the day shifts when he was at the surgery. And who was she to deny two small children a loving pet like Boy?

But her heart felt as if it were crumbling.

CHAPTER TWELVE

He didn't know what to do.

It was Christmastime and she was sad and she'd said she wanted to make happy Christmas memories. He didn't know how to make her smile. When he'd picked up Boy from her clinic the other day she'd pressed her lips together so hard he'd thought she might have drawn blood. Her brave goodbye to their puppy had splintered his heart. And even when she'd come to his place the next morning and they'd made love it had been heart-wrenching and desperate.

Yesterday had been the same. She was trying hard to be okay, but she wasn't. And now it was late afternoon on Christmas Eve and she'd had the day off to get ready for her move back… home. But she didn't seem happy about that either. He needed to make her smile. That was the thing about relationships, however burgeoning and new, or however old and familiar, however fleeting: you held each other up when needed. Beth needed holding up.

He found her at Bay View, sitting on her mum's bed looking at an old book, with a backdrop of so much glitter and tinsel and Christmas guff it made his eyes water. Someone here really, really liked Christmas. He was pretty sure it wasn't Beth.

'Alex?' The affection in her eyes made his heart contract into a tight ball.

'Ho. Ho. Ho. And all that.' Unable to stop himself, he went over and gave her a kiss that he knew looked a lot more than just good friends— which was the description she'd given her mother, apparently.

He kissed her mum too. On the cheek. 'Is it okay if I steal your daughter away for a few hours, Mrs Masters?'

'It's Hazel. You always called me Hazel before.' She patted his hand. 'Yes, I'm fine. Go. Go. We're just going through some old photos. I could sit here for hours and look at my little Beth. You want to see—?' She offered the book to him but Beth stopped her and rolled her eyes.

'Mum, no, he does not want to see what I looked like as a baby. I'm a grown woman.'

Hazel's eyes were filled with affection for her daughter, and a little motherly irritation. 'A grown woman who needs to get a life. Go.'

Alex managed the briefest of glimpses at the pictures. Beth sitting on her father's knee. A Christmas cracker hat almost covering his eyes. He laughed. 'I've seen those photos before. You were a very cute baby, but you're a hell of a lot cuter now.'

'What do you want?' Another eye roll. But her cheeks pinked and she smiled. Result! 'Where are we going?'

He walked her outside to his car, held the door open for her. 'I promised you a date. So here we are. Hop in.'

'It's so beautiful here in the winter.' She stared out of the window as they drove along the narrow winding road. It had stopped snowing a few days ago but was cold enough for the snow to stick. The leafless trees looked like strange eerie sculptures in a stark white landscape. She sighed. 'It's going to be a white Christmas.'

He wasn't going to think about what tomorrow was going to bring. 'Will you stay with me tonight?'

She blinked and looked at him curiously. Then nodded. 'Yes. Yes, I will.'

'And have you…' He didn't want to say it. Think it. Believe it. 'Packed everything for your trip back tomorrow?'

Her mouth tightened. 'Pretty much.'

Don't go. It was a selfish thought and he

pushed it back. There were so many things he wanted to say, on the tip of his tongue. So many words. He was going to miss her.

It was for the best.

I love you.

What the...? That one punched his chest, staccato. Like shots fired. I. Love. You. The shock was the same and had his brain reverberating. But she was talking and he had to pay attention. 'Oh, before I forget. Two things: June's gone to the foster home with Meg. She's going to be okay. And...the results came back on the food sample I took at Oaktree Farm.'

'Did it find anything?' He registered that June was okay. Great. And there were results. But his thoughts swayed back. He loved her. He'd asked her to stay the night when in reality he wanted her to stay for ever. He wanted to make her happy. But he couldn't. She made him happy and he didn't want that to end.

Selfish.

She was animated as she talked. 'They found traces of ibuprofen. So Dennis must have put it there. Luckily, Boy didn't eat enough of it to make him sick and the lavage would have washed out any lingering traces. It makes me so angry and sad that he was doing that. Why? Why would you do that?'

Now he was focused but the hollow feeling

in his chest lingered and his stomach clenched. 'My guess is that it was a cry for help. He was lonely and wanted to feel important. You remember how he perked up when we said he'd saved Meg's life? It made him feel useful. Will you report him?'

She nodded. 'I'll have to. Obviously.'

'If he survives the accident he probably won't go back to the farm. Chances are he won't be allowed to own any animals. It's an illness, Beth. Doing something like that is an illness.'

She shook her head. 'It's just so sad.'

'Poor guy, to be so desperate to do that. Poor animals.'

What else was pretty damned sad was that Alex had held back for eight years because he hadn't wanted to get to this damned point. Yet here he was. In love with her. Never stopped being in love with her. And he was still impotent to do anything about it.

They'd arrived in Carlisle and he pulled the car into the side of the road as soon as he found a decent parking spot. 'Looks like they've closed the road. We're going to have to get out and walk.'

She climbed out and when they rounded the corner she gasped. 'Wow. It's beautiful.'

Even he had to admit that the sight of dozens of little timber huts decorated in tiny white fairy lights and a carpet of twinkling snow was magical. 'I heard there was exceptional *glühwein* here. We have to find that stall.'

'Good plan.' She slipped her hand into his and they started to make their way round the stalls. They didn't get far before she'd slipped a red Santa hat, with flashing lights on the brim, onto his head and made him pose for a selfie. 'Say bah humbug, Alex.'

He got her back with a kiss under plastic mistletoe. And another under some of the real stuff. And another just because...

They ate mince pies and sampled limoncello and artisan fruit cake. A little brass quartet was playing Christmas carols and she started to hum so badly it made him laugh. Then he pressed her against a lamppost and kissed her long and hard and he had to admit that sometimes Christmas could be okay.

But he didn't wrap tinsel around her head and tell her she was his queen. And he certainly didn't propose as he had all those years ago. Although, the idea flickered in the background no matter how much he pushed it away.

He loved her and he was letting her know and letting her go. Again. That was his gift to her.

'This is the best *glühwein* I've ever had.' She licked her lips and turned away from the stall, accidentally bumping into a pregnant woman who was holding a baby that looked about a year old.

'Oh, goodness. I'm so sorry.' Beth cooed to the baby and smiled at the woman and made sure they weren't harmed. 'Oh, Laura, I haven't seen you for ages. How's things?'

'Beth Masters! Hello!' But the smiling woman rolled her eyes towards two-peas-in-a-pod toddlers who were running around and between their mother's legs. 'Oh, you know. Busy.'

'Twins? Lucky you.' Beth bent down and smiled at each of them, fishing candy canes out of her bag and, with the mum's nodded permission, handing them one each. 'They're gorgeous.'

'They are so competitive. You wouldn't believe.' Laura jiggled the baby on her hip. 'This one's learning to walk and I can't keep up with him. I hope this one's quieter.' She patted her swollen belly. 'A girl would be nice, but you can't choose, can you? How are you? You got kids?'

'No. No kids.' Beth's eyes darted over to him and he felt the burn in his chest. Her eyes were kind and yet tinged with sadness. 'I'm just here to play.'

'Lucky you.'

Beth ruffled the baby's head and beamed. 'No, you're the lucky one. Just look at that gorgeous smile.'

Then Laura headed away and Beth's eyes followed them as they wove through the market. Alex took hold of her hand and brought her to a stall selling organic soaps and candles, trying to reconnect with her. But she looked back again, so he asked, 'Old friend?'

'Someone from school. Can you believe it? She's my age with three kids and another on the way. Busy.'

'She doesn't know busy until she's got a puppy with authority issues.'

'Oh, Alex. I miss him.' She hugged him tight. 'I hope he's happy with his new family.'

'I'm sure he will be.' Not wanting to add to her worries, he didn't tell her about the three calls so far asking how to stop Boy chewing everything in sight.

Because, man, she had so much love to give, so much hope in her heart. She deserved to have a happy ever after filled with kids and babies and puppies under her feet. She deserved to fill her heart and her home with love and laughter and little ones. She deserved a row of stockings on the fireplace and late-night assembly of tricky plastic toys on Christmas Eve. She deserved all the love that came with excited squeals, and tinsel and glitter and Christmas magic. He didn't know what to do or say because he couldn't make her feel better about this. He was the wrong guy.

Thoughts tumbled and jumbled and reassembled in his brain and he put his hand to his head to stop them. But he couldn't. Truth was, this was just a game of trying to pretend there wasn't a massive elephant in the room. Playing at being a couple when it was never going to happen. He turned round, his boots making a dark, dirty circle in the snow. And another.

She caught his arm. 'Alex, what is it? What's the matter?'

'Nothing. I'm fine.' But he took her arm and gently steered her away from the crowds. He couldn't do this here. Not with the tinsel and Christmas music...

She shook her head. 'It's not fine. Stop. Talk to me. What's the matter?'

He stopped and put his hands to her face, wishing his heart weren't tearing open like a cheap Christmas cracker. Wishing it were May bank holiday or Midsummer's Eve and not bloody Christmas. 'I can't... Baby, I can't do this.'

She gripped his sleeve and stumbled back with him to the car. 'Don't. Don't, Alex. You promised me tonight. You promised.'

'Tonight and then tomorrow morning and then when would it stop? Glasgow isn't far away. We'd do the weekend thing, holidays. Then you'd move down here and we'd slide into something you wouldn't be able to say no to.'

He opened the car door and she climbed in. 'I don't understand. Are you asking me to stay?'

With a tight knot deep in his gut, he slid into

the driver's seat, stabbed the ignition pad and pulled into the night. 'No, Beth. I'm telling you to go.'

She shook her head sharply, her mouth wobbling. She pressed her lips together. Then, in a small voice, 'Why?'

'If I asked you to stay, I get the feeling you might say yes.' Keeping an eye on the road, he touched her cheek. 'And, God, there is nothing I want more. We're good together. We both know that. So damned good. You make me feel things I never thought I'd feel again. You make me... hell, Beth... I...'

He wanted to tell her he loved her. It was shining brightly in his head and his heart. But if he told her that she'd stay, out of misguided loyalty to a dream they'd once had and hope they might actually have it some time. He tried to keep his eyes on the road but kept being drawn to look at her. Luckily, the traffic was quiet, everyone with their families, enjoying Christmas Eve. Having fun.

She blinked. Fast. 'But—'

'We'd settle into something nice and we'd get comfortable and then one day you'd look back...like you did just then. You'd look back and see what other people had and you'd wish and then you'd wonder why you'd given up your dreams, for me. I saw the way you looked at those kids. The affection. The longing. You've always wanted a family, Beth. Hell, you deserve one. Don't you dare give up on what you want.'

'We could adopt. We could... I don't know, we could see someone, a specialist.' Her breathing was as frantic as the look in her eyes. 'We could...whoa. Be careful, it's icy.'

The car skidded and he fought for control, trying to slow everything down, not quite believing he was back breaking her heart all over again. So much for being gentle. He turned left onto the Oakdale Road. 'You want your own family. Your own babies. Don't tell me you don't. Adoption is difficult and not guaranteed.'

'You wanted children too, Alex. I know it's the end of a dream for you, not just me. You don't have to pretend you don't care because I know you do.'

Of course he cared. Caring hurt like a sharp knife being jabbed into his heart. Over and over. For eight long years. 'You can do it, though. You can go ahead and have your dream. With someone else.'

She opened her mouth, closed it. Tears glistening in her eyes. Then one fell. Another. 'We could just have pets. Dogs. A puppy.'

He looked at her as his heart shattered, wanting to stop her tears, wanting to promise her everything. 'Clutching at dreams, baby. A puppy is never going to be enough. Not even two. Three. A whole damned zoo.'

She swiped her sleeve over her cheek. 'So, this is it?'

'It was always going to be it. You knew that. I was honest from the start. You need to pin your hopes on someone else. Someone better.'

'There you are again, making decisions for me. I can choose, Alex.'

He pulled up outside her cottage. It was dark. There was no jolly Christmas wreath on the door, no welcoming lights. 'Don't choose me.'

'So what? You're going to end up all alone? Like Dennis? On purpose?' she shouted at him. Angry. Magnificent. Beautiful. Her fists on his chest, pressing, pushing. 'For God's sake. I don't believe you are doing this. After everything we've been through. Everything we've shared. I should never have let you into my heart again.'

Then she climbed out of the car and slammed the door.

Slamming shut the last chance of happiness he'd ever have.

How bloody dared he?

How dared he saunter into her life and break her heart all over again? She stumbled into the cottage and leaned back on the front door. Her old home was pitch black and empty.

Just like the way her life felt right now. She'd given part of herself to Alex and to Boy, the parts she should have given to someone who would have treasured them. Treasured her. And not thrown it all back at her.

She took a deep breath and shuddered on the exhale. Tried to control her inhale. And out. Tried to calm down. She was done. Done.

No. She was nowhere near done. She was raging.

She flicked on the light and stormed into the lounge. The pathetic Christmas tree she'd decorated with her mum sat in the middle of the floor like a bad omen. She ripped the baubles off and stuffed them back in their box, then picked up the tree, snapped the branches off and stuffed them into the last black bin bag she had.

Gone. Done. Done. Bloody Christmas. Bloody men.

A tear dripped onto the plastic. Then another. And soon a torrent of them fell, making rivulets on the bin bag drizzling to the floor. Why did it have to hurt so much? Why did she pick the wrong men? *Man.*

It was only ever Alex. He was the only man she'd ever loved.

Her fist closed round the bag and her fingernails dragged holes in the plastic. The truth flickered starkly, blinking like the lights on the Santa hat she'd made him put on for the photograph. Why did he make her hurt so much?

Because she loved him.

After everything he'd done to her the first time around, and still she'd opened herself to more hurt. She loved him. How could she have been so stupid? How could she have been so reckless with her heart? Again?

Loved him without a shred of sensibility. Loved him with abandon. Had pretty much offered up her heart and invited him to stomp on it. She stalked upstairs to her room, tripping over her suitcases on the floor, adding stubbed-toe pain to the physical hurt in her heart. She kicked one over.

Thank God she was leaving this place. Thank God she still had a house and a job in Glasgow. Thank God she hadn't given up her dream for him.

But what use was a dream if the man you loved wasn't in it, sharing it, loving you back?

CHAPTER THIRTEEN

THERE WAS FRESH snow to greet Alex when he opened the blinds on Christmas morning with about as much cheer in his heart as the Scrooge character he was often compared to. Not surprising, really, given that memories of Christmases past had done their very best to haunt him into the early hours.

He'd done the right thing. Twice. And that was it. He was never getting involved in a relationship again. Climbing and hiking, doctoring and sleeping. That was what his to do list was now. Nothing else. No emotions, no feelings. Certainly not falling in love.

He peered through the wooden venetian slats and watched the Oakdale locals milling about the village square in heavy coats and red and white hats, smiling, laughing, hugging. He shivered and shoved his hands deep into his pockets. Happy Christmas? Just another one to chalk up to experience. Next year he'd definitely go

somewhere else. Australia and sunshine sounded
good. Anywhere where he'd miss this.

A rap on the door made him jump. Beth? She'd
come back?

He flung it open and found Joe and Rose and
Joe's daughter, Katy, standing there in terrible
matching festive jumpers with reindeers on. Joe
held out his hand. 'Just passing, thought we'd
stop to say happy Christmas.'

Alex shook his hand. Surprised. Thoughtful
of them. But the last thing he wanted was to
pretend to be jolly when his heart was in pieces.
'Oh. Right. Thanks.'

Rose grinned and held young Katy under her
armpits as the girl's legs slithered on the path.
They were both laughing. Rose held Katy tight
and pressed her head to her stepdaughter's.
'Katy wanted to try out her new roller skates.
But they're not great on snow.'

'Not any better on concrete either. I don't think
it's the roller skates, I think it might be opera-
tor error.' Joe laughed. Then his smile dropped.
'You okay, mate?'

'Oh, you know. Fine.' He wasn't fine. This
was Joe's family's first Christmas together and
Alex was watching them all huddled together and
laughing and so…so much more than okay that it
made him feel worse…and had him wondering

how it could be that some people embraced the Christmas spirit and others just…didn't.

Then he thought about something Beth had said about making the most of it. Yeah. The only thing that would make him smile right now was seeing her face. It had been ten hours since she'd slammed that car door. Ten hours where he'd thought he'd feel better about breaking her heart. And maybe he did, just a little, because once again he'd done it for her own good. But not for his.

But the sad truth was, he didn't want to end up lonely. He didn't want to be alone. He wanted to love her. To have her in his life. Always.

He'd been too quick to dismiss her thoughts and suggestions. He'd mired himself in feeling sorry and spiritless and hopeless for so long he hadn't been able to grasp a chance at pulling himself out of it. He'd pitied himself for what had happened to him and for the loss of his dreams and had expected others to do the same.

He'd accused Beth of doing it when maybe… just maybe, she actually was attracted to him the way he was attracted to her. Their lovemaking hadn't felt like something she'd been doing because she felt as if she had to or because she wanted him to feel better. It had been hot, electric, intense, giving and taking in equal measure.

And he'd fallen for Boy within about two minutes of meeting him. Okay, perhaps it had been love at first sight. So maybe he could grow to love an adopted child too. If he truly loved Beth he could at least try.

Couldn't he? The same way Joe and Katy had let Rose into their hearts. The way she'd grown to love Katy as her own daughter. His phone buzzed in his pocket. He took it out, his heart swelling in the hope of seeing her name.

It wasn't Beth. But he nodded to his unexpected guests. 'Sorry, I'll just have to take this. Have a good Christmas, guys, and enjoy the skiing.'

They laughed and waved as he talked and listened. And when he flicked the phone back into his pocket he smiled. Maybe…just maybe… Christmas was indeed what you made it.

Beth had put on a brave face for her mother, but her heart hadn't been wholly invested in looking for a twenty-pence piece in her Christmas pudding, or singing 'Jingle Bells' and drinking lumpy eggnog, so she'd slipped away quietly after giving her mum a tender hug and promising to visit again soon.

To be fair, Bay View had put on quite a day of it and with all her mum's new friends fussing and laughing Beth had felt like a spare part.

She was glad to be alone in her car where she could...okay, wallow a little.

The drive to Glasgow was remarkably smooth and she pulled into her garage and sighed. She'd thought—hoped—that the sight of her house would make her feel better, that being back here would ease the ache, but it didn't. She was still angry that he hadn't been willing to hear her out. To consider options.

But at least the anger fuelled her muscles and she emptied the car of numerous boxes in no time. Then she switched on the central heating, made a cup of tea and sat in *her* lounge, in *her* house. *Her* home. One day it would feel like a proper home too. She was determined to make the best of it. One thing she knew she was good at was being kind to others and now she had to be kind to herself. She would heal in time. She had a job she loved. She had a lot more than some. A lot more than poor Dennis. Her heart twisted thinking about him and the dogs and her lovely Boy. And then, of course, her Alex.

Next Christmas she'd have a huge tree. She'd make it the best Christmas ever and put this one down to a memory she'd prefer to forget. Although, she would never, ever forget Alex. She just had to get over him. She sighed. She'd done it before. She closed her eyes and fought back the tears. No more. She was done.

Oops. Running a finger under her eyelid, she caught a rebellious stray tear. *Almost* done. She took a deep breath, blew out slowly and stood up. 'Right. Time to make a life.'

An hour or so later she was unpacking her suitcase when a hammering on her door had her heart racing. Who the hell would that be on Christmas Day? She didn't know the neighbours. Was it the police? Was her mum okay? She ran down the stairs and tugged open the door. Did a double take. Forced herself to breathe. 'Alex.'

There he was. By some miracle. On her doorstep, wearing the most ridiculous Christmas jumper, with embroidered red bells tied with a bow and the words 'Jingle My Bells' written above. And it wasn't fair, because even with that ghastly number on he looked so damned beautiful it made her heart stutter.

He smiled warily. Unsure. 'Er… Happy Christmas?'

'Christmas, yes. Happy? What do you think?' Her heart was now in overdrive and her body prickling with longing. She scooped some snow from the garden wall and cooled her face with it. His fancy-pants car was in the driveway and she could see something moving…no, jumping inside.

Her heart lurched. 'Oh? Is that…is that Boy? In the car? What's going on?'

Alex shrugged. 'It didn't work out with the family.'

'Why not? What was wrong?' Was he here just to dump the dog on her? Just the way he'd tried to a few weeks ago? Typical. It wasn't about her at all. It was about him. Business as usual.

'He wasn't happy, Beth. Not at all.' Alex's lips pursed and he looked as if his heart was going to break. 'He didn't settle. He just howled the whole time and scratched at the door. He chewed everything in sight and pooped on the Christmas presents.'

She bit back a laugh. Some people shouldn't have pets. 'They didn't give him much of a chance. Three days?'

'They tried everything but…well, he missed us and they didn't think it was right keeping him when he was so sad. They were so worried. But they've phoned round and found another puppy who loves them and does what he's told…at least some of the time.'

'And you've brought him here for me to look after, is that it? I only have a small place.' She pointed to her tiny hallway and imagined how quickly Boy would wreck everything within reach. 'It's not dog-proof. I can't—'

'Actually, I've decided I'm going to keep him. We kind of get along. I've given up all hope of ever having a pair of un-chewed shoes again. Or a rug that hasn't got teeth-shaped edges. I've arranged for Fraser's daughter to play with him while I'm at work. When she starts school I'll have a rethink. But I'll work something out. Frank's wife said he can go up there and play. Frank's home now, by the way—he called earlier to say thanks and to wish us all the happies for the season.'

'That's good. That's great. I'm happy for you all.' But her heart was breaking. It had been a kind of comfort to think he was hurting and alone too, but now…man and dog were together and she was… She took a deep breath. She was fine.

She would be.

'Do you want to see him? Before he claws holes in my fancy-pants upholstery?' Alex's gaze snagged hers and this time his smile was a lot warmer and hopeful and friendly.

'Of course. Yes. Of course.' What was this about, then? Had he come to show off? He'd got the dog and she hadn't? She watched as he walked to his car and as he opened the door a blur of brown streaked past and bounded towards her.

'Oh, Boy. Boy.' She knelt down and nuzzled

into his fur, her throat raw and sore. 'How was my baby on the journey? Did he howl and cry or was he a good boy?'

Alex's voice was pained. 'Howled, the whole way.'

She imagined that. And Alex trying to deal with it and drive. It would have been terrible. Boy could make a hell of a decent howl. 'Good. But at least he wasn't car sick.'

Alex's eyebrows rose. 'Ah…'

'Oh, good boy.' She fussed her puppy again. Fussed and scratched and rubbed and poured all her emotion into cuddles. Because here they were taunting her with her lost dream all over again and she didn't want to let it go. 'Vomiting on the fancy-pants car. Oh, who's a good boy? You're a good boy, aren't you, darling?'

Alex stood back and watched, a frown settled on his forehead. 'This is not going to plan. It seems like you're only interested in him.'

She stopped fussing and looked up at him. *Really?* 'Because he doesn't want to break my heart.'

He knelt down next to her. 'Neither do I, Beth.'

'It's a bit late for that, right?'

'Can we come in?'

Like hell. She wanted to scream at him, to show him her bruised heart. But he'd come all this way and he was smiling and there was just that little bit of hope and her hands were shaking and it wasn't all because Boy was here.

'I suppose so.' She scrambled up from the step, picked up Boy and walked through, hoping he'd follow. 'Five minutes.'

'That's all I need. Oh, and a lifetime.'

She whirled round to face him. 'What?'

He took a step towards her. 'I'm sorry, Beth. I was spooked by the emotions. I'd taught myself to stop caring because I didn't dare to think I could live our dream. It wasn't possible. It isn't.'

'But we can try. We can talk about it. Talk to specialists. It doesn't have to be your way or no way.'

'I know. I'll do anything, anything to give you the family you want. Adopt. Surrogacy. IVF…a sperm donor. All of it, none of it. Whatever you want. I love you so damned much, Beth. I've spent eight years trying to get over you and I just never will. No woman has ever been a match to you. You're my best friend, my lover. My love. I just want you in my life.' His eyes danced. 'And not just for Christmas.'

'You love me.' She had never seen anyone look at her the way he was looking at her right now. He didn't have to say the words, she could see it in his eyes, in the hope glittering there.

'I love you, Elizabeth Grace, with everything I have. I adore you. I miss you and I hate it with you gone.' He picked up the puppy and waved a paw. 'Don't we, Boy?'

She slapped her hands to her hips. 'You're using the puppy to get me back?'

He winced and winked. 'Desperate times. What can I say?'

'You broke my heart. Twice. I don't think I can get over that.' But she was willing to try. Because this was her chance. Her dream.

He loved her.

'I am going to spend every second of the next thousand years making it up to you. I promise.' He circled his puppy-free hand round her waist, loosening her grip on her hips, and pressed close. 'Please come back to Oakdale. Please, my love. Come back to your for-ever home.'

'Oh, Alex. Yes. Yes. I want to come home.' A tear escaped just when she'd thought she was done with them. But these were happy ones, so she didn't fight them. And when he lowered his mouth to hers she let him kiss her, totally and thoroughly, and things were just starting to get interesting when she felt a wet slurp on her cheek. She pulled away from her man and pressed a kiss to her dog's head. 'I love you. I always have. And by you, I mean both of you.'

'We love you too. Even more than chewing on state-of-the-art climbing shoes. Well…almost.'

Alex brought his mouth back to hers. 'Happy Christmas?'

She smiled, her heart full. 'Yes, my love. The happiest Christmas ever.'

One year later...

'Has he been? Has he been?' Little Leo tugged on Beth and Alex's blanket, breathless and so over-excited his feet danced over the carpet.

Beth opened one eye and her breath caught in her throat at the sight of her bright, funny, kind son. It had been a hard road but she and Alex had walked it together and last week they'd signed the adoption papers and become a family. She bit her wobbling lip and smiled. First Christmas nerves. She hoped she'd done it all right. 'Should we go and see?'

'Wait for me.' Alex shoved back the covers and bounded across the room, sweeping up the three-year-old into his arms and tickling his pot belly. As she watched them in cahoots and disappearing towards the stairs, Beth pinched the back of her hand just to check this was real. Because if it wasn't and it was just a dream, she didn't want to wake up.

Downstairs she was greeted by delighted squeals and a happy bark as Boy ran between their legs, not understanding what the fuss was

about, but knowing it was something special.
From behind, Alex wrapped his arms round her
waist and hugged her hard. 'I told you that tree
was too big. It's too tall for the ceiling and bent
at the top.'

She turned in his arms and kissed him. And
again. 'Alex Norton, hush your mouth. There
is no such thing as a too-tall tree. Or too much
Christmas pudding. Or being too happy.'

'And are you?' He tilted her chin so she could
see his eyes. So blue. So true.

'More than you could ever imagine.' She
leaned against his chest as the mayhem of torn
paper and more coloured plastic than was healthy
for a three-year-old littered the carpet. 'Are you?'

'Well, it is Christmas, so I have to be merry
and jolly, right? That's the law.' Grinning, he
pulled a little velvet box from his track-pant
pocket and held it out. 'But I will be very happy
if you say yes.'

'What?' Hands shaking, she took the box. *Another pinch me moment.* So many lately. And
opened it. Inside was… A lump filled her throat.
'Oh, Alex. Is this…?'

'The ring I bought you all those years ago.'

It was still the most perfect, beautiful, stunning diamond ring she'd ever seen. And she
loved it. Had always loved it. There weren't
enough words. 'But I thought… I decluttered it.'

'You did, but apparently your mum salvaged it and let me know she had it. *Just in case...*' Smiling, but also a little uncharacteristically nervous, he took her hand. 'This is my just in case, Beth. This is my everything, my wish. My dream. Will you marry me?'

It was her dream too. Always had been. She just couldn't believe it was finally coming true. 'Oh, my goodness. Yes! Yes, I will marry you, my darling man. Oh, Alex, I love you, so much.'

He crushed her against him; she could feel his heart pounding. A jolly, merry kind of beat. 'Then I am the happiest man alive.'

* * * * *

*If you enjoyed this story, check out
these other great reads from
Louisa George*

Saved by Their One-Night Baby
A Nurse to Heal His Heart
Reunited by Their Secret Son
The Nurse's Special Delivery

All available now!